CHILDREN OF PROMISE

CHILDREN OF
P·R·O·M·I·S·E

T. L. TEDROW

JUL   1996

THOMAS NELSON PUBLISHERS
Nashville

Published in Nashville, Tennessee, by Thomas Nelson, Inc., and distributed in Canada by Lawson Falle, Ltd., Cambridge, Ontario.

While this book is a fictional account of Laura Ingalls Wilder's exploits, it retains the historical integrity of her columns, diary, family background, personal beliefs, and the general history of the times in which she lived. However, any references to specific events, real people, or real places are intended only to give the fiction a setting in historical reality. Names, characters, and incidents are either the product of the author's imagination or are used fictitiously, and their resemblance, if any, to real persons, living or dead, is purely coincidental.

Library of Congress information

Tedrow, Thomas L.
    Children of promise / T.L. Tedrow.
        p.   cm. — (The Days of Laura Ingalls Wilder ; 2)
    Summary: In 1905, Laura's assignment to write an article for the Mansfield, Missouri, newspaper about the new school teacher leads her to start an unpopular crusade to get the farm children into school.
    ISBN 0-8407-3398-4 (pb)
    1. Wilder, Laura Ingalls, 1867–1957—Juvenile fiction.
[1. Wilder, Laura Ingalls, 1867–1957—Fiction.   2. Frontier and pioneer life—Missouri—Fiction.   3. Farm life—Missouri—Fiction.   4. Missouri—Fiction.]   I. Title.   II. Series: Tedrow, Thomas L. Days of Laura Ingalls Wilder ; bk. 2.
PZ7.T227Ch   1992
[Fic]—dc20   92-10141
                                                                 CIP
                                                                  AC

Printed in the United States of America
        ‾ 4   5   6   7   —   96   95   94   93   92

To my pretty wife Carla and our younguns,
C.T., Tyler, Tara and Travis.

May we never forget the magic of childhood dreams which
is really what being young at heart is all about.

And to my good friends at Thomas Nelson,
for making these dreams come true.

CONTENTS

FOREWORD

Laura Ingalls Wilder is known and loved for her pioneer books and the heartwarming television series based on them. Though much has been written about the old West, it was Laura Ingalls Wilder who brought the frontier to life for millions of young readers.

The American West offered a fresh start to anyone brave enough to face the challenges. These people tamed the frontier, crossing the prairie in wagons carrying furniture, seeds, and children, looking for a place to build a new life. They went west to raise families, build farms and towns, churches and businesses. They went knowing they would face hardship and danger, but that those who survived would have a future for their children.

Laura Ingalls's adventures did not stop after she married Almanzo Wilder. She went on to become a pioneer journalist in Mansfield, Missouri, where for sixteen years she was a columnist for the weekly paper *Missouri Ruralist*.

Laura Ingalls Wilder, a self-taught journalist, always spoke her mind. She worked for women's rights, lamented the consequences of war, and observed the march of progress as cars, planes, radios, and new inventions changed America forever.

While this book is a fictional account of Laura's exploits, it retains the historical integrity of her columns, diary, family background, personal beliefs, and the general history of the times in which she lived. However, any references to specific events, real people, or real places are intended only to give the fiction a setting in historical reality. Names, characters, and incidents are either the product of my imagination or are used fictitiously, and their resemblance, if any, to real-life counterparts is purely coincidental.

T. L. TEDROW

CHAPTER 1

FALL IS IN THE AIR

The lonely, wild cries of Canadian geese heading south came early to Apple Hill Farm in the fall of 1905, either a sign of hard times or a hard winter to come.

As evening descended over the Ozarks, Laura felt a tinge of jealousy, watching the geese fly overhead. They were leaving for another home, another place, another state. They had no thoughts of exactly where they were going; they were just going with inborn direction and a sense of purpose.

The flight of the geese reminded her of her own family's search for the perfect home all over the prairies of America. Each journey began with great promise but ended somewhere between happiness and heartache.

Laura was thirty-eight years old now, sitting on the fence between youth and old age. The time had come for her to put aside regrets and "what if's" and accept life as it is and will be—to make the best of each day.

The geese honked overhead in a symphony of joy. The leaders of the V-formations sounded out to the followers, who honked their response. Like arrowheads flying through the clouds, the geese flew over Apple Hill Farm, leaving Laura behind.

If she could have taken flight with the geese, Laura would have lifted her arms and flown with them for a short distance, just to regain that feeling of independence that only pioneers understand. She would let the wind take her to the ends of the earth and back again for no other reason than to just go . . . to just do it.

Though she had married a farmer who was tied to the land, she had been raised as a pioneer girl and still longed for the prairie days, when each new morning birthed a different adventure. Laura loved Apple Hill Farm, but would never forget the feeling of living one day at a time in a wagon-house on wheels, staying here for two days and there for a week because the fishing and hunting were good. Rolling through an endless prairie of days that stretched toward eternity, and nights where Pa played fiddle songs that seemed to stitch the stars together as she fell asleep on his lap.

Though Apple Hill Farm was wonderful, there had been other moments in her life when it could not have gotten any better. If she closed her eyes, Pa's fiddle notes could be heard dancing on the leaves.

The geese honked overhead, flying with their necks outstretched. They announced to the world that they were on the move again. It was an irresistible call that could not be ignored.

Laura stood on the highest hill above the farm and watched the leaders calling out to their followers. What had Manly once told her? *Everything is lovely when the geese honk high*? Something like that.

Soon the lakes and ponds in the Ozarks would be filled with Canadian geese and their smaller cousins, the mallards, black ducks, wood ducks, pintails, and even some canvas-backs. The river marshes would have mergansers and coots, and the farmers would have their shotguns in hand, harvesting meat from nature's storehouse.

The sight of these wonderful creatures gave her peace of mind. It was as if the world was coming alive through the sounds in the air . . . sounds that seemed to be saying to Laura, *Life will go on. All things shall pass.*

Maurice Springer, their black neighbor, sometimes laborer, and friend, trudged up the hill to where Laura was standing. His steps showed every one of the forty–five years he'd been on this earth. The lines on his face were etched with a thousand aches and pains.

"Those geese makin' you dream too, Laura?"

Laura closed her eyes and hugged herself. "Oh, yes. I can close my eyes and be a million miles away, floating on the evening breeze."

Maurice looked at the black-faced geese flying over-head and sighed.

Laura whispered, "And where do you want to dream away to, Maurice?"

"Sometimes black folk want to fly away to a beautiful land . . . back to Africa . . . where we could be people again."

"Is that what you want?"

"Sometimes. You see, Africa is some black folks' dream place. It was our land before freedom came to us here. We ain't never goin' back 'cause we ain't part of it now. But that don't mean we can't dream about what it might be like."

Laura could understand. "I dream about my childhood home on the prairie all the time. I know it's gone and I'll never see it again, but my memory carries the smell of Ma's cooking and the sound of Pa's fiddle songs." She closed her eyes and dropped her head, deep in thought.

Maurice understood, but he wanted her to understand him. "You been to your dream place, but I ain't never been to Africa. Look at this," he said, pulling a crumpled old picture from his wallet.

It was a picture of a group of black people, tired, with a wary, defensive look in their eyes. They were staring straight at the camera, a black couple in ragged clothes with a plump baby in the woman's arms.

"That's my folks after they tried to escape Mr. Cunningham's farm in Winchester, Virginia."

"Is that you?" Laura asked gently, pointing to the plump baby boy.

"Yes. Mr. Cunningham gave this picture to me when freedom came. He put it in my bag and gave me five dollars and a train ticket to St. Louis, to be with my momma's sister."

"What happened to your parents, Maurice?" Laura asked quietly.

Maurice looked away as if the pain of losing them was still sitting on the edge of his heart. "My folks died in the fightin' when the Johnny Rebs were retreatin'. The town of Winchester changed hands seventy-seven times durin' the war, and they were killed durin' the last go 'round."

Maurice stopped for a moment and rubbed his eyes, then shook his head and smiled. "So that's how I got to Missouri."

Laura watched him look into the distance, seeing everything but looking at nothing in particular.

He turned to her and said, "White folks don't know what it's like to live, get by, just going along day by day. Knowing that you're always goin' to be looked at for the color of your skin and not what you are inside."

Laura looked down, not really knowing what to say. "That's not fair, Maurice. We're not all that way. Aren't we friends?"

He shook his head like a person does when trying to wake up from a nap. "Sorry, you're right. I was just judgin' all white folks as one and the same." Maurice paused for a moment, then said, "But sometimes I wonder if those black-faced geese ever dream of Africa too."

CHAPTER 2

BUILDING A FIRE

Manly Wilder left the two geese he'd shot on the front porch. He wanted to get a fire going in the parlor because there was a chill in the air.

The late spring and cool summer had delayed apple picking for most of the growers in Wright County. For the first time that Manly could remember, they hadn't begun picking the Apple Hill orchards until late September.

Throughout the Ozarks, most of the fruit was hanging tight, not dropping early. The cool late-summer nights had given the apples a deep color and unusually good flavor.

Manly believed that an early winter was coming and had already picked and sold most of his crop. The rest he was holding for local sales, personal use, and canning. Anything left over would go to the cider press.

Most farm mortgages depended on the yearly crop, and Manly had urged everyone in town to bring theirs in early. Those farmers who were flirting with Jack Frost were tempting fate to make a little more profit.

His philosophy on apples was simple. A farmer hoping to cover his mortgage would be a fool to leave the fruit on the trees until they'd fully ripened. There was no way you could bring in a crop of fully ripe apples, prepare them for shipping, and get them to market before they spoiled. Harvesting earlier was a compromise between full flavor and profit.

Manly had patience developed from maturity and hard knocks. They'd lost their farm in the Dakotas by betting against Mother Nature, so now he was content to play it safe and plan for next year.

Living with Laura also took patience. She was outspoken, headstrong, and willing to stand up for herself. Though women weren't allowed to vote, what she advocated in her columns for the *Mansfield Monitor* influenced people throughout the region.

Manly loved her, despite all her opinionated ways. Laura had accepted becoming a farmer's wife when what she had really wanted to do was travel. And Manly accepted Laura's voicing her opinions, even though he had come to believe that sometimes silence was truly golden.

That's why he enjoyed building the fire without her sitting in the corner rocking chair trying to direct the show. Just as too many cooks can spoil the soup, there should be only two feet planted in front of the fireplace when a fire's being built.

"Mine!" he said out loud.

Jack the dog raised his head and looked at him. "Think I'm crazy for talking to myself?" he said with a laugh to the dog.

Manly reached to open the flue. The chain was stuck, so it took a moment to work it free. He thought he heard bats in the chimney but wasn't sure.

Spreading the andirons out, he laid two thick logs parallel. On top of these he placed two thin logs, running perpendicular. It looked like a log house on top of the andirons.

Under the logs he filled the center with dried grass, old newspaper, and a stack of sticks of various sizes from the copper holder next to the fireplace. He balled the newspaper up so that it would burn easily.

With some larger pieces of kindling, Manly built a teepee under the log house, carefully adding progressively larger pieces. When he finished, the unlit wood looked like a pyramid.

Rolling a piece of newspaper tight, he struck a wooden match and lit the paper. He held it like a torch and stuck it into the opening he'd left in the pyramid.

As the fire reached upwards, catching perfectly, Manly sat back to admire his handiwork and enjoy the first blast of warm air.

You can't ask for much more in life, he thought to himself, looking at the firelight dancing around the room. Manly had built the house with his own hands and had made the fireplace with rocks from the property.

Life is good on Apple Hill Farm, he decided as he walked outside to take the geese he'd shot to Laura.

Up on the hill, Laura saw the sparks flying up from the chimney. *Manly must be in a good mood,* she thought to herself.

Looking at Maurice, she asked, "Do you know that no bird has more than four toes?"

Maurice scratched his chin. "That a fact?"

"Sure is."

A long V-formation of Canadian geese flew overhead. Maurice looked at the honking birds and turned to Laura. "Those geese got toes?"

"Yup, that's right."

Maurice shook his head. "I don't think so."

"What don't you think?"

"Those geese only have one web on each foot. Ain't got no toes."

"But that counts as one toe."

"In what book does it say that a spider spins a toe? He spins a web."

"Oh, Maurice, you're just being silly."

"Me?" he said, with a sly grin on his face.

"You want me to tell you something?" Laura asked. Maurice nodded. "I learned a poem about birds in school when I was a little girl, so I could remember how to call geese and ducks properly."

"When I hunt a duck, all I say is 'quack-quack' and 'bang-bang' with my shotgun." He began laughing again.

"Maurice, will you just listen? I want to tell you my poem:

> Geese on the ground are a gaggle,
> Geese in the air are a skein,
> Ducks on the ground are a paddling
> And ducks in the air are a team."

Maurice rubbed his stomach and added:

> "And geese on my plate are great,
> and ducks in my tummy are yummy!"

He belly-laughed and slapped his knee.

Manly, who had never regained his health after a crippling stroke in the Dakota Territory, limped up the hill, carrying two fat geese.

"I shot a couple of nice ones on the creek." Handing one to Maurice, he said, "Take this to Eulla Mae and tell her she owes me one of her blueberry pies."

Maurice took the fat bird. "He's a big one! I know hunger doesn't regulate the time of day, but this fat bird makes my hunger clock tick faster. Think I'll just take him home and get Mr. Goose dressed for dinner tonight."

"Want me to send along my prize dressing recipe?" Laura asked.

"No, but thanks. Eulla Mae makes the best cush 'round. Why, she takes that Indian corn and works it into a thick dough with chopped-up onions, some pepper, salt, greens, carrots, and whatever else she feels like and sticks it inside Mr. Goose."

"Stop it. You're makin' me hungry!" Manly joked.

Manly pointed down the ridge to the fence on the next hill. "Be careful walkin' on the path in the dark. I was fixin' the fence, and I might have left some boards with nails stickin' up."

Maurice lifted the goose into the air. "If you step on a rusty nail, you just put some goose grease on the nail and drive it deep into the east side of a sycamore tree."

"Why?" Laura asked.

"To stop infection." Laura saw mischief in Maurice's eyes. "Learned that from the hill doctor when I was little."

"Watch your step anyway," Manly said.

As Maurice walked down the hill toward his farm in the next hollow, Manly put his arm around Laura. "It's getting dark, and there's a chill in the air. Let's go on back to the house. I started a fire in the parlor for you."

All around them, crickets were calling one another to come out and sing. Manly took off his hat, wiped his brow, and handed her the goose.

"Laura, I brought you this fine goose for a reason. I'm hungry!"

Laura laughed, "Okay, you silly goose, let's go start this bird. But you have to pluck and dress it. That's not part of my duties."

Before he could answer, she tossed the goose back to him and skipped ahead, whistling. Manly responded, but several V-formations of geese overhead drowned him out.

Laura called back, "What did you say?"

"I said, 'A whistling woman and a crowing hen don't never come to no good end.' "

Laura called back, "Grab the feathers, pull 'em loose, who does the pluckin' is the goose!"

Her laughter echoed off the hills as she raced back to the house.

The aroma of the roasting goose kept Manly sniffing most of the night, and he awoke in a grouchy mood.

He turned to Laura and said, "I still don't understand why we couldn't have just sliced it up last night and eaten it."

Shaking her head, Laura said, "You've got to roast a goose overnight."

"Why? Why couldn't we just eat it and let it sit in our stomachs overnight? Maurice got his goose cooked!"

Placing her hand on Manly's shoulder, she said, "Goose is a dark meat and needs to roast a long time. The fatty bottomside bastes the bird, and with the stuffing I made, you'll be glad you waited."

Manly sniffed the air and pulled on his socks. "What did you stuff it with?"

"Mashed potatoes, apples, onions, spices, and . . ."

"Stop it. You're killing me!" he interrupted. "I'm going to have a headache all day thinkin' about that goose waitin' to sit on my plate and smile up at me all juicy like, wantin' me to chomp on his tender little drumstick feet."

"I'll make you and Rose a big country breakfast," she said, heading toward the kitchen to start the coffee.

Manly licked his lips and hurried down to the kitchen. "You always know the way to my heart."

After breakfast, Laura had to keep watch on the oven all day, because Manly came up with dozens of things he needed to do in there and couldn't be trusted not to pick at the roasting goose.

She finally sent him into town to invite Andrew Jackson Summers, her boss and the editor of the *Mansfield Monitor,* to dinner. His wife and son were away visiting relatives, and he'd all but invited himself to dinner twice this week alone.

Manly pouted about going to town. "I still don't understand why you don't just call him on the phone."

" 'Cause I want you out of the house. You're sniffing around like a starving dog."

As Manly left for town, he turned and asked, "You sure there's enough goose for all of us?"

"There will be, if you don't pick the bird to death."

After inviting Summers, Manly rode back to the farm and slipped into the kitchen without making a noise. By mid-afternoon, there were so many pick-and-poke holes in the goose that it looked like Swiss cheese.

CHAPTER 3

THE NEW TEACHER

Andrew Jackson Summers came riding up on his horse at exactly 7 P.M. He was a big, rotund man, always hungry and always ready to talk about what he wanted to talk about. With his wife and son away, he'd jumped at the chance to come eat a home-cooked meal.

His newspaper had been started with a press, paper, ink, type, coffee, and a pistol to keep unhappy readers at bay. The original editorial staff didn't have any writing experience when Summers bought the paper from its cranky first owner, so just printing articles without grammatical errors and with sentences that were clearly written was a vast improvement over what the paper had been like for years.

Laura had a unique position with the *Mansfield Monitor*. Since the paper couldn't pay her much, she just wrote about things that concerned her.

It was the best of both worlds, because it gave her the opportunity to address issues and problems that concerned her without being tied down to a desk every day.

Occasionally Summers would ask her to write about a local person or happening, but generally he left her pretty much to her own devices.

"Evening, Laura, Manly," Summers said, tipping his hat as he came up the stairs.

Summers looked at Laura and Manly's daughter, Rose. "You're a mighty lovely gal, Rose Wilder. I bet you've got all the boys' eyes at that high school in New Orleans," he said.

Rose, a seventeen-year-old beauty, blushed. "Oh, Mr. Summers! I hardly have time for boys."

With a wink of his eye, Summers laughed. "Rosie, all work and no play can even make you a dull girl."

"I've set my sights on being a good newspaper writer, like my mother."

Summers laughed again. "If she's as good a cook as she is a writer, then my hunger will be taken care of."

Manly looked at Summers's waistline. "Looks like it's been taken care of a number of times already."

Summers waved his hand and passed the comment off. "Just the jealousy of a skinny man."

"Come on in, everyone. Even this skinny man needs to eat," Manly said, holding open the door.

Laura and Manly sat at the head and foot of the table, while Rose and Summers sat facing each other.

Summers sipped his water. "Rose, your mother is a great undiscovered writer. I think that one day she'll be so famous that I won't be able to afford her, which is why she accepts what I pay her now."

"I'm not sure how to take that," Laura said, laughing. "Will you say the blessing for us, Andrew?"

"It'd be a pleasure," Summers said, sniffing the wonderful aromas of the roasted goose and smiling as he looked over the food spread before him.

Laura watched Summers during dinner, knowing that something was on his mind. It usually took him a while to get to the point, so Laura just sat back and waited until he was ready to say whatever he was going to say.

Summers mentioned the new school year that was just beginning, and for a time everyone at the table reminisced about their old school days.

It was all just polite conversation. Laura knew that Summers was leading toward something. This was the way he handled all his interviews and warded off bill collectors.

"And did you know," Summers finally said, wiping his lips and pushing his plate forward, "that there's a new teacher taking over the elementary school?"

"Had a new one last year, didn't we?" asked Rose. "What happened to her?"

"She got married to the sheriff over in the next county," Manly answered.

"I hope the teacher is a good one," said Rose. "Is she new to the area?"

"Not only is she new to the area, this teacher is also new to America!" Summers exclaimed.

"So," Laura said, "there must be ten million new Americans around here nowadays."

"Does she speak English?" Rose asked.

Summers stammered, "Yes. Well, sort of, but . . ."

"Sort of?" Laura questioned.

Summers pushed his chair back and stood up. "Her name is Maurene O'Conner and she's from Ireland and . . ."

Laura put her napkin down. "And what?"

". . . and she's an Irish Catholic."

"Is she here to teach religion or elementary school?" Laura quietly asked.

"Why, she's here to teach school," Summers said.

"Is she pretty?" Laura asked.

"So pretty that she reminds you of shamrocks, Irish linen, and Waterford crystal all wrapped up in green and topped with flowing auburn hair."

"I'd like to see her. Ouch!" Manly blurted out, after a swift kick to his ankles from Laura.

Manly rubbed his ankle and snorted, "About half of Missouri is Catholic."

"Not Irish Catholic," Summers protested.

Rose jumped in. "There's German Catholics in the middle of the state, French-Canadian Catholics over on the river, and Irish and all kinds of Catholics here in Mansfield."

"I know that!" Summers said. "But we've never had a Catholic teacher in Mansfield. I even got a letter from the Klan about it." The table was quiet for a moment.

"What did they send you?" Laura asked, her voice as cold as ice.

Summers pulled a folded broadside from his coat

pocket. "I don't agree with this, but you got to pay attention to all views in this business."

"There aren't two sides to everything in this world," Laura said, unfolding the paper that Summers handed her. "Sometimes there's just right and wrong."

BEWHERE! WARNING!
KATHLICS ARE TAKING OVER YUR SKOOL!
DO U WANT YUR CHILD TAUGHT BY A KATHLIC?
DON'T LET THIS AGENT OF THE POPE CONVERT YUR CHILD!
FRUM THE GRAN DRAGON OF THE OZARKS

Laura crumpled the paper and looked at Summers. "You should have just thrown this away."

"They got a right to say what they want," Summers said.

Manly snorted. "But the right thing to do is not to pay it no mind."

"This is nonsense," Laura said, helping Rose pick up the dishes and take them to the kitchen.

Summers talked to her back as she went into the kitchen. "Laura, go interview her. Find out what she's like. You've got a good nose for news. Maybe you can reassure the town and stop any trouble before it starts."

"It doesn't matter if the public-school teacher is Methodist, Episcopal, or Baptist! The question should be, is she a good teacher!" Laura spun around, stamping her feet. "Worrying about a Catholic teacher when most of the kids in these hills can't even spell the word *Catholic*!"

Summers shook his head and smiled. "You're a hard one to argue with, and that's why I print your blather!" He stood up, folding his napkin. "It was a wonderful meal, but I've got a newspaper to put to bed, so I'd best be going."

"Thanks for comin'," Manly said, handing Summers his hat.

Adjusting his hat at the door, Summers looked into Laura's eyes. "You'll check this woman out for me?"

"Andrew, it's hard for the best and smartest people in the world to get along without a touch of decency. You don't have to agree one hundred percent with people to respect them as people."

"But you'll do a story and talk with her tomorrow?"

"I will."

Summers nodded his head in thanks and closed the door behind him.

CHAPTER 4

NEW MEMBERS

Sitting behind the roadside livery stable, halfway between Mansfield and Norwood, three men played mumblety-peg.

One was tall and thin, and the other was stocky and short. The third—the leader of the other two and the Grand Dragon of the Ozarks chapter of the Klan—had dark, bushy eyebrows that added to the intensity of his stare.

"Hey boss, you almost put the knife in my shoe," the thin man said, moving his foot from the edge of the circle.

"If you move your foot again, I'll put the knife in your leg," the Grand Dragon said. "Put your shoe back on the line."

The thin man reluctantly moved his foot forward and closed his eyes.

"Open your eyes, I ain't gonna hit your foot," he said, flicking the knife. It landed right against the heel.

"That was close, real close," the stocky man grinned. "Do it again."

"Put your own foot up there," the thin man growled. "See how you like it."

The Grand Dragon stood up and walked over to the crude wooden table beside the horse stall. He picked up the top copy from a stack of Klan literature and read it over, then stamped his foot.

"What's eatin' you, boss?" the stocky man asked.

"We need some new Klan members . . . some dues-payin' members."

The stocky man scratched his head. "You got us two as members."

"And we got them three fellers over in Norwood who sometimes show up at the meetings."

"They only come when I'm buyin' drinks at the saloon."

"But that's six men . . . how many more you want?" the thin man asked.

"We need more. The St. Louis Klavern has almost five hundred in their group," the Grand Dragon said, furrowing his eyebrows.

"Takes money to recruit," the thin man said.

"And we don't got any money," the stocky man said. "With no blacksmithin' business to speak of, we can't go out seekin' recruits."

"And we only got three sheets and three hoods anyway," grinned the thin man.

The stocky man laughed. "Those Norwood boys

looked silly in them striped sheets. Kind of looked like zebras."

The Grand Dragon kicked the side of the horse stall, knocking a board loose. "We can get more sheets. Even if we have to steal them off a wash line, we can get more sheets."

"You got a plan?" the stocky man asked.

"I'm workin' on one. But we got to do somethin' to get some new members."

"Like what?" the thin man asked.

"Like attract some attention."

"We've been handin' out them papers like you told us," the thin man said.

"And we left that message at the newspaper office like you told us," the stocky man whined.

"And that's not enough!" snapped the Grand Dragon.

He picked up his knife and cleaned the dirt from the tip of the blade. The stocky man looked at his friend and rolled his eyes. "What're we goin' to do?"

The Klan leader shot his booted foot out and pinned the thin man's hand on the ground, then flicked the knife between the outstretched fingers. The blade wobbled back and forth, nicking the thin man's index finger and drawing blood.

" '*We*' ain't gonna do nothin'! *I'm* goin' to figure out a plan for us," the boss said, pulling his knife from the ground. He held the blade with the drop of blood up to the sun and smiled at the reflection.

"We're gonna make hay outta this new Irish teacher. We're gonna call a rally to run her out and recruit us some dues-payin' members in the process." He looked around the old barn. "Yessir, boys, by the time we stir things up, we'll have enough money to get us an office like they got in St. Louis."

"They got a telephone, I hear," the thin man nodded.

The Klan leader ignored the man's comments. "We'll get the loggers over on Hardacres Hill blamed for somethin' and scare the folks that their kids are being converted or somethin'."

The two men looked at each other, then the stocky man spoke. "Them Hardacres men are pretty rough. Can't we just do some night ridin' and scare some old folks? That'll get attention."

The Grand Dragon turned and stared intently at the two men. "No, let's turn Mansfield against itself. Catholic against Protestant. Irish against everyone else. It worked for the Klan in Virginia, so it should work here."

"I like it," smiled the stocky man.

"You always can think of somethin'," the thin man grinned.

"That's why I'm the boss. Let's get to work."

CHAPTER 5

MUCKROSS ABBEY

Maurene O'Conner, the auburn-haired beauty from Ireland that Andrew Jackson Summers was so curious about, looked in the mirror, fixed her hair one last time, and sighed. *It's a long way from the Emerald Isle to Missouri,* she thought to herself.

She looked out the window at the simple homes in the Hardacres, the section of town the Irish immigrants of Mansfield had claimed as their own.

America was nothing like she imagined. Oh yes, she'd been warned about the rough-and-tumble ways and that the Irish were generally disliked. What she hadn't been prepared for was the general lack of concern for education in this rural area.

She came to America to escape the poverty of Ireland and to forget about her heartache. In a frame on the dresser was the pressed leaf of a potato plant.

It's funny, she thought to herself. *A simple vegetable plant has changed the world.*

Christopher Columbus had brought the potato back

from South America to Europe, where it became a major food staple. It was easy to grow and could feed a lot of people cheaply. Along with the potato crops, the population of Europe burgeoned.

In Ireland, the people became completely dependent on the potato to feed their families. The potato was so essential to the survival of the growing population that when the potato famine of the 1840s hit, the only hope of survival for hundreds of thousands was to leave Ireland.

The Irish would never forget that the British failed to help them with food during the famine. While thousands were dying of starvation, the English closed their eyes and ears to the pleading families seeking food.

So the Irish headed across the Atlantic and forever changed America in ways both known and unknown for years to come. They were restricted to the bottom of the ocean-crossing ships, crammed into the interior rooms without windows. When the *Titanic* sank in 1912, some of the Irish families were locked in the bottom so the other passengers wouldn't have to share lifeboats with them.

Prejudice against the Irish as a nationality and against their religion was so strong that in America they were kept from living in certain areas, eating in some restaurants, doing certain jobs, and were refused admission to clubs and organizations.

The noise of children playing and dogs barking made Maurene O'Conner sigh. She had her work cut out for her. She hadn't been taught how to teach Americans at her school in Ireland.

She looked around instinctively for the religious symbols that were on the walls at her home near Ring of Kerry. Ah, did she miss that beautiful place just two miles across the old wooden bridge from Muckross Abbey. If her parents were alive, she would never have left. After they were gone, however, there was nothing for her in Ireland except heartache and painful memories.

She looked at the picture in her gold locket Michael McGuire, the dashing man she had been so in love with. Packed inside her trunk were his love letters. The memories flooded back as she lifted them out.

Her plans to become Mrs. Michael McGuire had ended in a skirmish with British soldiers near Muckross Abbey. She and Michael had been minding their own business, walking from the town with fresh bread they'd bought, when they were caught in a crossfire.

She winced at the thought of the day that had changed her life forever. While Michael lay dying in her arms, she'd begged God not to take him. But God had made up his own mind and took Michael home.

She had asked for God's help and guidance as they lowered Michael McGuire into the ground. She had trusted him to lead her and had ended up in America, in Mansfield, Missouri.

She was a long way from Muckross Abbey. Under Lord Cromwell in 1652, the British had burned Muckross Abbey down, and it had become a symbol of

the battle between the British crown and the Irish Catholics—a battle that inflamed religious prejudices.

This had happened over 250 years before Maurene O'Conner had come to America, but Maurene could see it had planted seeds that grew even in American soil. She saw it in the eyes of the lads from the Hardacres and those from the Protestant part of town.

She was staying with Wiley O'Reilly's family in the Hardacres Hill section of town. Free room and board was listed as a job benefit, but only because teachers weren't paid enough to afford their own food and housing.

The Hardacres was where the Irish loggers and day laborers lived. Their children were known as rough kids, and the non-Catholics of Mansfield looked down their noses at them.

Because of the prejudice against them, the kids fought back. They had been born into a fight that was already hundreds of years old and would probably go on forever.

That's why the Irish were so excited about having an Irish teacher and the Protestants of the town were uneasy. The Hardacre kids felt that Miss O'Conner wouldn't look down on them and their homespun clothes and hand-me-downs.

For the Protestants, it was time to worry that the shoe was on the other foot and hope that what goes 'round didn't come 'round.

Maurene O'Conner looked out the window at the Hardacre children outside. Some were on their way to school, and some were going with their fathers to work at the logging mill. She'd argued with the O'Reillys about keeping young Wiley in school.

His father thought it was time he "earned his keep," but Maurene had convinced him to let Wiley spend another year in school so he could learn how to read.

She was going to be the only teacher at the school where children ranged in age from just under five to twelve. "You'll need the luck o' the Irish," she laughed aloud to herself, as she headed off to her first day of school.

CHAPTER 6

MORNING AT THE YOUNGUNS'

ut I'm a boy."

"No, you're not," Sherry Youngun laughed. "You're a father!"

Rev. Youngun, minister of the town's Methodist church, sat there exasperated, wondering how to deal rationally with a five-and-a-half-year-old daughter.

Soaking wet from trying to bathe her for the first day of school, he looked at Dangit the dog, peeking out from under the sink. Dangit followed the three Youngun children everywhere and looked like a cross between a mutt and a double-mutt.

With a white paw, one bent ear, a crooked tail, and a black ring over his left eye, Dangit would let you do anything to him except misuse his name. If you stubbed your toe and screamed "Dangit!" by mistake, he'd rip the cuffs off your pants!

Sherry slipped and splashed water onto her father. He wiped it off and asked God for patience. Being a widower and raising three kids was no easy job.

Rev. Youngun sat looking at his daughter, standing in front of the old washtub with the towel half-wrapped around her.

"Ma told me *boys* shouldn't see me neck-ed," Sherry said loudly. "She didn't say fathers were boys."

Drying off her hair with the end of the towel, he quietly said, "The word is naked, not neck-ed, and fathers were once boys."

"No! You were not!"

He started chuckling at the absurdity of the situation. "I'm sorry, but I was once a little boy."

"I'm sorry too, but I don't believe it!" Sherry said, putting her hands on her hips.

Her seven-year-old brother, Terry, stuck his head inside the kitchen door, and she screamed, "Get outta here!"

Terry ran down the hall laughing. Rev. Youngun shouted after him, "I told you boys to stay out of the kitchen until Sherry is dressed."

"But we're hungry, Pa," came ten-year-old Larry's voice from the parlor.

"We'll be only a few more minutes." Turning back to Sherry, he was taken aback to see her with the towel wrapped around her little waist, wiggling around.

"Sherry, what are you doing?"

"Terry taught me this. 'There's a place in France where the ladies do their dance and . . .'"

He clamped his hand over her mouth. "Hush!" She tried to wiggle away, but he held tight. "Terry, get in here!"

Terry came in sheepishly. "Yes, Pa?"

"Did you teach Sherry that?"

Terry looked at Sherry, who was wide-eyed and red faced. "Teach her what, Pa?"

"You know."

Terry shook his auburn-crowned head. "No, I don't, Pa."

Rev. Youngun suddenly thought about the pretty widow, Carla Pobst, whom he'd met during the summer of 1905. They had corresponded, and he had seen her several times when she had come to visit. She had gone back to Cape Girardeau to settle her affairs and promised to return by New Year's.

Though they'd only gone buggy riding, he found himself thinking about her often. It was lonely trying to raise these three children by himself, and he missed talking and laughing with another adult around the house.

Thinking about another woman made him feel guilty, so he looked up and addressed his wife, who had died of the fever last year. "Norma, why can't you be here?"

"Cause she's dead, Pa." Terry said. His lip began to flutter.

Rev. Youngun turned on Terry, thinking he was being disrespectful. "If I wasn't a minister, I'd smack you!" Then he saw Terry's tear-filled eyes and caught hold of himself. Terry was only reacting to his comments about his departed wife.

He picked up Terry and smoothed his hair. "Son, all

I'm trying to do is straighten things out. I miss your mother too. I miss her every day."

Placing Terry back down, he asked calmly, "Did you teach Sherry the you-know-what dance and song?"

Larry was hiding around the corner, nodding his head. Terry reached around the doorjamb and bopped him a good one on the arm.

"What's a you-know-what dance and song, Pa?" Terry asked, all wide-eyed and innocent.

Rev. Youngun stood up, let go of Sherry, and began dancing. "This dance." As he wiggled his hips and hummed the tune, Terry broke up laughing.

Sherry's towel dropped so she screamed, "Get that boy outta here!"

Rev. Youngun figured he looked pretty foolish and shooed Terry from the room. "Get your dress on right now, young lady."

She picked up the dress with a sinking frown.

"Now what's wrong?" he asked, wiping some of the water off the floor.

"Sometimes I wish I was a boy."

He stared at her. "First you tell me you don't like boys, and now you tell me you want to *be* one! That doesn't make sense, little girl."

"Well, if I was a boy I wouldn't have to wear dresses and I wouldn't have to go into the outhouse. I could just go on a tree, like Terry does."

"No, I don't, Pa!" came the unasked-for response from the hall.

Rev. Youngun looked at his daughter. "God wanted

you to be just the way you are. You're the sweet little Missouri apple of my eye."

"Yeah, you look just like a crab apple," Terry laughed, poking his head around the corner and sticking his tongue out at her.

"Pa, he said I look like Crab Apple the mule!"

Terry ran off, screaming, "Roses are red; apples are too. Sherry is ugly, and looks like a mule!"

Rev. Youngun dashed out in the hall and caught Terry by the seat of his pants. Sherry took the opportunity to slip her old workpants under her pink dress. She just wanted to be ready in case there was some boy-stuff she wanted to do!

Meanwhile, ten-year-old Larry was in his room feeding his various caged bugs and snakes. There were black snakes, lizards, box turtles, spiders, and boxes of bugs on the wall that he'd caught and collected throughout Wright County. He knew more about bugs than just about anyone around and seemed to always have a crawlin' this or that in his pocket.

Kids called him "the bugcatcher" because he could identify anything that crawled. Some of the boys liked to tease him by squishing bugs and lizards in front of him, but most folks respected the knowledge he had.

Terry, who shared the room with Larry, seemed to collect trouble and mischief. He had—hidden under the bed, behind the bookcase, and under the mattress —tricks and traps like hand buzzers, whoopee cushions, jumping snakes in the can, and generally anything available that would make girls scream.

He once paraded through town with a pair of red
long johns that he'd found at the dump. Told everyone
they had belonged to Davy Crockett and if you had a
penny, he'd let you touch them. All the kids lined up
and Terry told a whopper of a tale about how "old Davy
Crockett himself had worn these old long johns when
he kilt himself his first bear."

Terry made himself fifteen cents before Sheriff Sven
Peterson came to stop him. The sheriff was really a
softie and didn't even like to carry a gun since they'd
never had any violent crime in Mansfield.

Thomas Huleatt, who owned Tippy's Saloon, named
after his birthplace, County Tipperary, Ireland, happened up and listened. Terry talked the sheriff out of
telling his father about the Davy Crockett underwear
caper and into letting him keep the fifteen pennies in
his pocket.

Huleatt thought Terry was one heck of a grafter, so
he gave him a quarter for the red underwear and
pinned them onto his saloon wall. He told Terry that he
could have a job dealing poker when he grew older if he
wanted to.

Larry took out a three-foot green snake and turned
to his brother. "You shouldn't have taught Sherry that
France-girlie dance you heard in town."

"She just shouldn't have done it in front of Pa. I
can't be blamed for educatin' her," Terry snipped back.

"That's cute," Larry said, "always makin' excuses."

"Breakfast, boys," shouted their father from the
kitchen.

"I wonder what Pa's tried to make this time. A kid could starve to death 'round here, with his cookin'," Terry said, taking out his hidden pocketknife and sneaking it into his pocket. He called it his "just-in-case" knife and carried it everywhere.

"Come on," Larry said, racing from the room. "Let's eat fast, or we'll be late for school."

The two boys raced to the kitchen, bumping into their father, who was juggling a tray of cold cornbread and sliced cheese that one of the parishioners had given them.

"Slow down, you two!"

"Sorry, Pa," they both laughed.

The three Younguns took their places around the table, with Sherry sitting on the embroidered pillow with her "blam blam" blanket and her doll, Carrie Nation— named for the famous crusader against liquor—resting on her lap.

"Pa, she's sucking her thumb again!" Terry exclaimed.

"Am not!" Sherry answered, pulling it from her mouth.

Rev. Youngun shook his head. "You're going to look like a beaver and eat corn through a picket fence if you keep sucking your thumb."

Sherry started crying, and it took him several minutes to calm his daughter down. He looked at their scrubbed faces and brushed hair. *Thank heavens, school's starting back,* he thought to himself.

At the end of the meal Rev. Youngun poured each of

them a healthy dose of castor oil. While he cleared the table, the three kids carried their teaspoons of what Terry called "liquid death" onto the porch. Larry put his teaspoonful into his mouth, just like Pa had told him to. Terry made a terrible face at the thought of the taste.

"You got to take it," Larry said. "It's good for you."

"You're right! And this will be good for you, too!" Terry said, offering his teaspoonful of the foul-tasting stuff to his brother.

"You got to drink it," Larry smiled, walking into the kitchen.

When their brother was out of sight, Terry and Sherry held their spoons for Dangit to lick.

"It's good for you, Dangit," Sherry smiled.

"That's what I call a good dog," Terry said, heading toward the kitchen.

Dangit ran from the porch, swinging his head around, trying to get the taste of the castor oil off his tongue.

CHAPTER 7

HARVEST TIME

As Laura walked along toward the old schoolhouse to meet the new teacher, she was amazed at the beauty around her. Leaves were turning in a brilliant display. Summer was leaving, and the first frost of autumn was in the air. Like the geese honking overhead, the frost was on its way.

The *Farmer's Almanac* had predicted an early frost with a very cold winter to come. Like their neighbors around them, the Wilders were stocking up food for the winter, repairing the fences, and bracing the roofs and porches against the predicted heavy snows to come.

Laura and Manly swore by the *Farmer's Almanac,* which forecasted the weather for American farmers. In the Ozark hills, where a good newspaper might be several days old, predicting the weather was always an inexact science. Farm crops could be lost if they weren't in by first frost and since the *Farmer's Almanac* was something that could be counted on, no one asked or really wanted to know how it came up with its predictions.

The little book, with the hole in the corner for hanging on a nail in the barn, was filled with all kinds of curious, useful, and useless information. It became a national sensation when it accurately predicted snow in New England in July of 1816.

Abraham Lincoln used the almanac in a successful defense of a client who had been accused of shooting a man by the light of the moon on August 29, 1857. Lincoln held up a copy of the *Farmer's Almanac* which showed there wasn't enough moonlight on that date to shoot anything.

The jury took it as gospel, and so did millions of Americans.

Farmers were busy in the fields, trying to bring in the crops before they were ruined. They all had either read the almanac or had it read to them. Added to that were the geese-filled skies which had followed the swarms of monarch butterflies heading to Mexico from Canada.

The seasons were changing. Laura could feel it in the air and hear it in the sound of the crunching leaves underneath her feet. A gust of wind brought a flurry of multicolored leaves from the trees above her. They raced in swirls, some flying in bands and others seeming to play follow-the-leader before diving to the ground.

Laura smiled. Single leaves spiraled down in quick

descent, while others drifted along on invisible breezes like ships at sea, sailing boldly over the trees.

It was harvesttime in the Ozarks. Another season was about to change.

CHAPTER 8

NEW SHOES

Larry, Terry, and Sherry Youngun helped rinse the breakfast plates and put them away. While their father got ready for another day of ministering, the Youngun children looked for their old shoes.

They weren't there! All they could find were three pairs of new shoes—three pairs of strange-looking, shiny new shoes.

"Pa," Terry screamed. "Someone stole our shoes and left us some dancin' shoes. Guess we can't go to school today."

Rev. Youngun came out onto the porch. "How do you kids like 'em?"

The three children looked at the odd-looking shoes with straps, buckles, and higher-than-normal heels.

"Well?" he asked when no one spoke.

"Where'd you get 'em?" Larry asked.

Their father told them that the shoes had been donated to the church by Mr. Johnson, the desk clerk at the hotel, who had unusually thick glasses. Seems Mr.

Johnson had found them and brought them to Rev. Youngun after he saw his kids kicking cans in town with shoes full of holes.

As the children looked at the shoes, Rev. Youngun said, "I think you'll be the talk of the school in these shoes."

"You can guarantee that," said Larry quietly.

As the kids tried them on, their father gave them reassurance. "With a shoehorn and some paper stuffed into the toes, they'll be just fine."

It was time to go to school, so they sat on the front steps, looking at their new school shoes. The shoes were a shiny leather, not like the normal shoe-boots that farm boys in the area wore.

"What kind of person would wear these? A clown?" Terry said, shaking his head at the shiny shoes on his feet. "Can't climb no tree . . ."

Rev. Youngun corrected him. "That's any tree."

Terry continued, "Can't climb no tree or any tree in these stupid-looking shoes."

Rev. Youngun didn't want to tell him that the shoes had come from a traveling stage show which had played the town a few months back.

"They hurt, Pa," moaned Terry.

"New shoes always do," Rev. Youngun said, handing his son a shoehorn and not wanting his squirrely son to have any reason to miss school.

Larry inspected his stiff, new shoes. "They look like dancing shoes. Kids are going to make fun."

"They're fairly special for shoes," he said to his son.

Terry poked his brother in the ribs. "What he really means is that they're special sissy shoes. All the kids are going to make fun of us."

Rev. Youngun lined them all up at the door, hugging them close. "Try hard and be good. You've got a new teacher in the class and . . ."

"She's a Catholic leprechaun," snickered Terry.

"They look like leprechaun shoes," Larry said.

Sherry jumped back. "Are these what Catholics wear? And what's a leprechaun?" she asked.

Terry said, "I hear the new teacher is from Ireland and is a leprechaun. You know, those green little Irish cats with spots."

Larry interrupted him. "You're thinking of a leopard."

"What's a leopard?" Sherry asked.

"Where did you hear this?" Rev. Youngun asked.

"Some of the Hardacre kids were dancin' 'round singin' 'Barney, Barney, we're into five-leaf clovers,'" Terry said.

"That's 'Blarney' not 'Barney,' and four-leaf clovers, not five," Rev. Youngun corrected him.

"Why were they singin' about barns?" Sherry asked.

"They weren't, dummy," snapped Terry. "Pa, since you're a minister, do you believe that a Methodist missionary goes to heaven and a cannibal goes to the other place?"

Rev. Youngun was half-listening, fixing the bow in Sherry's hair. "Yes, I believe that. Methodist missionaries should go to heaven."

Terry then asked, with a deadpan face, "But what happens if the Methodist missionary is in the cannibal's tummy? Do they both go to heaven?"

It was another Terry trap, which Rev. Youngun decided to ignore. "Go on. Get going, now. You'll be late."

"What's a cannibal?" Sherry asked.

Rev. Youngun ignored her, shaking his head. He shooed them off the steps. "Walk straight to school and straight home. No monkey business."

"Can we stop at Willow Creek Bridge and swim on the way home, Pa?" Terry asked.

"No, the creek's cold and too deep this time of year. I want you all to come straight home."

"Bye, Pa," they all shouted, skipping off down the driveway with their dog Dangit yipping behind them. Sherry had to stop a couple of times to roll her pants legs back up, but she managed to keep up with her brothers.

Once around the bend, Terry began scratching under his armpits like an ape, trying to scare his sister.

Larry bopped him on the head. "Pa said no monkey business."

"Monkey this," Terry laughed, kicking Larry and racing ahead for dear life. He got far enough up the road so they wouldn't see him eat part of his lunch.

With a mouth full of food, Terry looked down at the round fruit on the ground, covered with sharp quills or horns. He looked up at the sweet gum trees with their brilliant fall foliage and stooped down to pick up a few of the sweet gum balls.

He put the three best in his pocket and then took another bite of his sandwich.

Larry and Sherry were still behind him, walking and talking together. Sherry got on her tip toes, "Want to hear a secret?" she asked Larry.

"Okay, but don't shout in my ear."

"I won't." Sherry put her lips against his ear and let a loud burp.

"Dangit, don't burp in my ear again!" he said, wiping her spittle from the side of his head.

Dangit the dog came running up and grabbed him by the pants leg and spun him around. He did that anytime someone used his name the wrong way.

"Stop, Dangit. Let go!"

They played tag and leapfrog until they got to Willow Creek Bridge and the fork in the road leading into town. One fork went to the Hardacres and the other into the high ridge section.

"Let's skip school and go swimming," Terry suggested. No one paid him any attention. They remembered what Pa had said.

Across the bridge was Thomas and Silvia Leidenburg's apple farm. They had two children, a nine-year-old son named Janson and a six-year-old daughter named Sil.

Thomas Leidenburg had a bad reputation in town. He kept his children out of school most of the year to work their farm and orchards, had a vicious temper, and drank.

Janson was picking apples and putting them in a

sack slung from his shoulder. He bit into an apple that was tree-ripened sweet. There was water in the core, which meant that the whole crop had to be sold locally because they wouldn't last for shipment to St. Louis or Little Rock.

His sister Sil was searching through the Jersey black apples that had dropped to the ground during the night. Some were still good, so she put them in her basket.

"Hey, Janson," Larry shouted. "Aren't you going to school today?"

"No," Janson said in his distinctive Swedish accent, "my father don't want me going with the apple harvest upon us."

"Lucky you," said Terry. "Wish my pa was like yours."

"No, you don't," said Sil quietly, as she climbed up the ladder.

"Hush, Sil," her brother said. "Here," he shouted, tossing an apple to Terry.

Terry caught it and skipped around. Janson tossed two more, and the Younguns left, waving and eating their apples. Terry, always wanting to be different, sliced his with his pocketknife.

"Want me to bring your assignments to you?" Larry asked.

"Naw," answered Janson. "Pa don't want me thinkin' about school."

Larry didn't believe him but let it pass.

"Bye, Janson. Bye, Sil," they shouted, skipping and running toward school.

They passed other children working in the orchards and fields.

"Some kids got all the luck," Terry mumbled to himself.

Janson and Sil watched the Younguns walk away toward school, wishing they were going.

CHAPTER 9

THE LEIDENBURGS

Thomas Leidenburg was having a bad morning. He'd had too much to drink the night before. He sat at the kitchen table, rubbing his head. His wife, Silvia, put away the breakfast dishes as quietly as she could.

Breakfast had literally been eat and run. Janson and Sil Leidenburg knew that if they didn't get out of the house before their father woke up, they might get a wuppin'. That's why they ran out without washing or fixing their hair, grabbing what they could from the icebox and eating their fill from the apple trees.

"Where are the kids?" he growled.

"They're in the orchards, working like you told them to, but I still think they should have at least gone to the first day of school."

"Farmers don't need to read and write. They just need strong muscles."

"They missed most of last year, and with a new teacher . . ."

Cutting her off, he said, "I've heard about this new

Irish teacher. They don't like us Swedes, and we don't like them. I don't want you to talk about educatin' Janson and the girl. Janson's goin' to follow in my footsteps, and Sil just needs to know how to cook."

He tossed away an empty bottle and began rummaging through the cupboards.

"No, Thomas, no!" she pleaded.

He stopped and glared at her. "Tell me where the money is."

Terrified of his rages, she pointed to the bottom cabinet. "It's inside the big cookpot."

Slamming open the cabinet door, Thomas pulled out the money and laid it on the table to count it.

"But that's all the money we've got left," Silvia whimpered.

"I'll earn enough from the apples this year to buy everything you need. Leave me alone!"

She grabbed his arm. "Don't do this. The whiskey's making you do crazy things."

All he could think about was getting to town and having a drink. "I told you to leave me alone!"

He tried to slap her, but she ducked and grabbed at the money.

"Give me the money, Thomas. Don't ruin the family anymore!"

"Stop your mouth!" he screamed and rushed from the room. He needed a drink, and nothing would stop him.

CHAPTER 10

PORCUPINE EGGS?

The children of Mansfield always got to school early so they could play games and gossip before classes started. As with kids everywhere, most told their parents they wanted to go early to study, but only a few ever cracked a book.

Little James, a cousin of Maurice and Eulla Mae Springer, was leading a game of "Did You?" on the school playground. Most of the kids were gathered around him, answering his call like a chorus.

"Did you go to the henhouse, child?"

"Yes, sir!" the kids shouted back.

"And did you get any eggs from the nest?" Little James shouted out.

"Yes, sir!" the kids responded, dancing around Little James.

"And did you make me eggs and ham?" Little James asked, licking his lips.

"Yes, sir!" the kids shouted.

"Then why am I as hungry as I am?" Little James laughed, not able to keep the game going.

Terry Youngun watched from the side, then motioned a couple of his buddies to follow him over to the side of the school steps.

As the children argued over who was going to be the next ringleader in the game, Terry was talking quietly with Sweet Tooth Martin, the son of the town's baker, Li Sung, son of Chan the Chinese store owner, and Frenchie, son of Lafayette Bedal, who owned Bedal's General Store.

"Can you keep a secret, Sweet?" Terry asked seriously.

Sweet glanced around, sure he was about to hear something bad or naughty. Frenchie and Li gave Terry a skeptical look.

"You know I can, Terry. You know I can," Sweet whispered.

"I got something here that's worth its weight in gold," Terry said, looking around.

Frenchie, Li, and Sweet leaned forward. "What you got?" they all asked in unison.

Terry reached into his pocket and took out the sweet gum balls that were covered with sharp quills. He covered them with both hands, looked around to make sure no one was looking, then said, "I got some porcupine eggs."

"Porcupine eggs!" Sweet said loudly.

Terry transferred the "porcupine eggs" to one hand and put his other over Sweet's lips. "Quiet, I only got

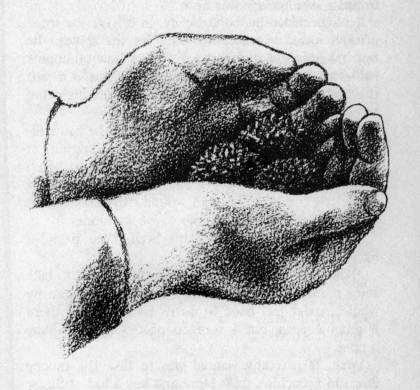

three. If the other kids hear, they'll all want 'em. I was goin' to sell 'em to you first."

"Let me see 'em," Sweet whispered, looking around to make sure no one was near.

Terry unfolded his hand slowly. In it were the three prickly, round sweet gum balls. "See the spikes," he told the three wide-eyed boys, "that's how porcupine babies are born. When the spikes get like this, it means they're turnin' into quills and the porcupines are going to hatch soon."

Terry was telling such a good story that he had half-convinced himself. "Ouch," he said, pretending one of the eggs had pricked him. "They're going to hatch soon. Zoos in St. Louis will pay through the nose for these." He turned and looked around. "Only reason I'm sellin' 'em is that I need some new-baby money."

"Baby money?" Li shook his head. "You havin' a baby?"

"Naw, there's a new baby in town that I want to take some money to. Just like to do it 'cause it will make my whole insides feel good to do it. I hate to sell these porcupine eggs, but I sure do need some new-baby money."

What Terry really wanted was to take the money down to Frenchie's dad's store and buy a bag of Sugar Baby candy.

Terry looked around and lowered his voice. "You got any money on you, Sweet?"

Sweet reached into his pocket and pulled out a handful of crumbled doughnut and three pennies. "I got three cents!" he said proudly.

"Good, but you keep the crumbs." Terry looked around again, lowered his voice, and spoke in his most convincing tone.

"How much they cost?" George asked.

Terry looked at the three cents in Sweet's hand. "Two cents each or three for three cents."

Sweet looked at the porcupine eggs. He said, "I'll take one," and handed Terry two cents. He took the porcupine egg carefully in his hand.

"How 'bout you two? You want one?"

Li and Frenchie each pulled out two pennies and handed them to Terry. If they'd thought it through, by pooling their money it would have only cost them one cent each, but they hadn't paid much attention to math lately, so Terry now had six cents, enough for a bag of Sugar Babies and two Tootsie Rolls.

"Class is starting. Everyone inside," an auburn-haired woman shouted, ringing the bell on the outside wall.

"Who's that?" asked Li.

"That's the new teacher," answered Frenchie. "Come on. Don't want to be late on the first day!"

Sweet stood up, flashing his porcupine egg. "I'm going to show this to the new teacher!"

Terry's eyes got wide, and his face went flush. Before Sweet could take more than a step, Terry pulled him aside and looked at the three boys.

"Don't tell anyone about this. Take them home and

hide them in your closet and don't think about it until they hatch. Could be a day or could be a year. That's the way it is with porcupine eggs."

As Terry started to leave, Li said, "Terry, you certainly come up with some unbelievable things."

"If you liked that, sometime I'll bring you some of Davy Crockett's hair."

CHAPTER 11

SCHOOL DAZE

The pretty, young teacher clanged the bell outside the door. Twenty-two students, ranging in age from just under five to twelve years old, came running and took their assigned seats by age groups.

Laura slipped in and sat in the back, observing the first day of school. Memories of the primitive schools she went to across the prairie flooded back. The bright-eyed, hopeful girls with clean, pressed dresses and pigtails were images of herself, years ago.

More than half the class was absent, home working in the fields. It was an accepted way of life in rural America.

"Sit down, sit down," Maurene O'Conner told the students. "School has started."

"I got to go," said Terry, heading out the door.

As the children settled down and squirmed in their seats, the teacher looked over the sea of scrubbed faces looking back at her. Some were wearing new store-bought clothes, and others were wearing hand-me-downs, with patches that needed patching.

It took a while for the class to come to order. The Younguns were sitting on the bench in the back, along with their pal Little James, watching Frenchie make embarrassing air noises with his hand under his arm.

Sherry began giggling. Terry was making faces through the window. Larry just shook his head and mouthed, "No!"

Laura watched it all from the back of the room, wishing she could discipline some of the children.

In the next row was Johnny, son of Stephen Scales, the telegraph operator. Johnny had been afflicted with a disease called polio, which had left him lame and dependent on crutches.

Next to Johnny was Ezekiel Wechter, the son of a rug merchant. The Wechters had come to Missouri from Russia by way of the B'nai Israel Synagogue in Pensacola, Florida, which had been home for the Wechters' relatives and other Jews for more than two hundred years. The Jews of Pensacola, Florida, had fled New Orleans in 1763, to escape persecution after the Treaty of Paris, when France's Louisiana Territory was given to Spain.

Ezekiel—everyone called him Zeke—wore a crocheted skullcap—a yarmulke—on his head, which the kids called a "beanie." He was the only one in class who got to miss school for the Jewish holidays *and* Christmas and Easter.

Across from Zeke sat Li. He was a good friend to the Younguns.

In front of Li sat Scotty, the son of Scottish immigrant Thomas Campbell, who owned the town's feed store.

A country girl had her eye on Larry and said she was going to marry him one day. Her name was Missouri Poole, the Okie daughter of the hill people.

Though Missouri was a pretty girl, Larry could never stomach the thought of having a girlfriend who smoked a big, old corncob pipe!

In the front row sat Sweet. George had a sweet tooth. His father, the baker, said that Sweet was the reason he never made any money! Sweet was the one to bet on in the county fair pie-eating contest.

Laura watched the antics around her and remembered her days as a sixteen-year-old teacher. Those were awful times, trying to lead a class of children who were almost her own age.

"Class, come to order," Miss O'Conner said as the children wiggled and giggled.

"At night she turns into a leprechaun," Li whispered to Larry.

He spoke just loud enough for Laura to hear, so she tapped Li on the shoulder. "That's not polite," she whispered. Li mouthed the word, "Sorry," and turned back to face the front.

Terry Youngun came skipping in from the outhouse. "Did everything come out all right?" sneered Red

Shaughnessy, one of the Hardacre boys, who'd been nicknamed for his flaming carrot-topped hair.

"Looked just like you," Terry snickered, sticking his tongue out. Red snarled and hit his palm with his fist.

"Are you a leprechaun?" Sherry Youngun asked, making the room snicker.

"Let me see if I've got my green shoes on," the teacher smiled, looking down at her feet. "No, guess I left my leprechaun shoes at home with my bag of treasure."

"What's a leprechaun?" Sherry asked.

"Want me to tell her?" Zeke asked.

"Shut up, smarty pants," growled Red.

"Why did you ask me if I was one, if you don't know what one is?" Miss O'Conner questioned.

" 'Cause I heard my dumb brother Terry say you were one," Sherry said as Terry sank down in his seat.

Miss O'Conner smiled. "Well, when I was growing up in Ireland, children believed in leprechauns the way many children like to believe in fairies. A leprechaun is said to be an elf who works as a cobbler and supposedly has lots of hidden treasure." Miss O'Conner looked around.

"Are you rich?" Sweet asked the teacher.

"Naw, she's Irish Catholic. They're poor," Little James said, without thinking.

Laura suddenly felt sorry for the teacher and what she was going through. *How can she control her temper over such rude remarks*? Laura asked herself.

Maurene O'Conner closed her eyes. *Muckross Abbey. The religious battle is still going on,* she thought.

"My name is Miss Maurene O'Conner, and I'm from . . ."

Sweet interrupted her. "My pa says you're from Ireland."

"Shut up," snarled Red Shaughnessy, one of the Hardacre boys.

The teacher smiled. "That's all right. Yes, I'm from the Emerald Isle and I'm . . ."

"Catholic," piped up Missouri Poole in the front row.

"And what do you know about Catholics, young lady?" Miss O'Conner asked. She'd been warned to expect this.

"They don't eat meat on Fridays," said Missouri Poole, looking the teacher straight in the eye.

The teacher smiled. "Yes, we don't eat meat on Fridays."

"I told you she's a Catholic," whispered Little James to Frenchie.

"So am I," whispered Frenchie. Little James looked surprised.

"You boys should be ashamed of yourselves," Laura whispered over Little James's shoulder.

Miss O'Conner looked at Laura and said, "Will the visitor to our class please refrain from talking to the students, or are you a new student?"

Laura was clearly embarrassed. "No, . . . I . . . I'm just observing. Sorry." *Here to check up on me,* thought Miss O'Conner, feeling irritated.

Terry raised his hand. "Does that mean that Catholic cannibals can't eat on Fridays?"

The Hardacre boys were grumbling, whispering among themselves. "We'll get you," mouthed Wiley O'Reilly to Terry, who whispered, "Get this," and shook his body and fist.

Miss O'Conner was trying to take it all in stride. "I suppose you know about the tribe of cannibals who were converted to Christianity by the Catholic missionary."

"Is that true?" asked Chubbs. "Are there Catholic cannibals?"

"How 'bout it, boy?" Gene Buchanan whispered to Little James. "Weren't your grandparents cannibals?"

"Didn't my grandfather own your grandfather?" snickered Wiley.

Miss O'Conner walked over and stood in front of Gene and Wiley. "Boys, stop that! That kind of talk will not be tolerated in my classroom!"

The two boys from the Hardacres looked down. "Sorry, Miss O'Conner," they both said.

As Miss O'Conner walked back to the front of the room, Gene Buchanan shot a piercing glare at Little James and Terry. Terry stuck his tongue out and snuggled closer to his big brother. Sherry looked down and saw that one of her pants legs was hanging down, so she quickly rolled it up.

"What about the converted Catholic cannibals?" asked Frenchie, Catholic himself, and interested in what sounded like his first history lesson of the year.

Miss O'Conner answered with a straight face, "Well, now, on Fridays, this tribe can only eat fishermen."

All but the little ones got the joke.

The teacher smiled. "I'm Catholic, but during school hours, I'm your teacher. You worship your way, and I will worship my way." She looked around the room. "Does anyone have a problem with this?"

"Why did they send a Catholic here?" asked Rudy Summers, the editor's son.

Laura winced in the back at what Miss O'Conner was going through. "Rudy Summers, no, no!" she whispered loudly.

Miss O'Conner looked at Laura. "You will have to be quiet, or you will have to leave. I am perfectly capable of handling my own classroom."

"Sorry," Laura said quietly. "It won't happen again."

Maurene O'Conner looked at Rudy Summers and answered bluntly, "I came here to teach young children and enlighten their minds. What I can't teach are manners, which is something you all should have learned at home." She paused and looked around, catching the eye of each student. "It's time for the flag salute. Who would like to lead it?"

All the children in the class suddenly went mute.

"Come on, doesn't anyone in this class know the pledge of allegiance?"

Sherry Youngun raised her hand.

"Okay, young lady, come up here and lead the class."

As Sherry proudly walked forward, a few of the kids snickered as her workpants unrolled under her dress.

Larry closed his eyes and shook his head. Terry put his head on the desk. This could be embarrassing!

Sherry looked at Old Glory and saluted with her hand on her forehead, as she'd seen soldiers do. "I pledge allegiance, to the flag, of the United Plates of America, and to the re-plub . . . re-plub." She always got stuck on that word.

Terry stuck his head up and shouted, "Republic!"

Sherry took it all in stride. "Thanks, Terry. And to the re-pub-plic to which it stands, one nation, under God, invisible, with liberty and judgment for all."

Miss O'Conner tried not to laugh when Sherry broke out singing her version of *The Star-spangled Banner.*

"O say can you see-saw, by the sun's early night, what so crowded we sail, in the twilight steamin'." The kids around the room shrugged their shoulders not knowing what she was singing.

"Sounds like the Star Mangled Banner," Larry laughed.

"Sounds *awful*," Terry moaned.

"Shut her up," snapped Frenchie.

Larry popped him. "Quiet . . . you're talkin' 'bout my sister."

Sherry, unaware of their snickering, jumped up on the bench near the blackboard and belted out, "Oh, say does that star sprinkled banner yet fly . . . over the land of the free, and the home of the grave."

Miss O'Conner shook her head and tapped Sherry on the shoulders, "Thank you, dear. That was certainly a different version. Thank you, Miss . . . Miss . . ."

"Sherry. Sherry Youngun. Can I go to the out-house?"

"Well, yes, go on, but be quick about it." Sherry skipped out of the class with her pants legs hanging down below her dress. "Now get out your McGuffey readers, and I'll test each of you to see where you fit in the class."

Laura would have helped, but she knew this was not her job. Miss O'Conner seemed very self-assured and might not appreciate Laura's trying to help.

After testing the children and moving them to rows with matched abilities, Miss O'Conner wrote on the board the pages of their McGuffey readers that each was supposed to read during this semester.

"I will accept no excuses. When I give you home-work, I expect it to be done."

"But what about our after-school work at home?" Missouri Poole asked.

Miss O'Conner just shook her head. "Anybody can clean a barn, but if you want to learn about the world and have a chance to move forward, then you must study."

"I don't want to leave the Ozarks," said Missouri.

"That may be so, but I will not accept farmwork, store work, or housework as an excuse. You may have to get up earlier or stay up later to get those chores done, but I expect your schoolwork to be done. That's the way we were taught in Ireland!"

The children were grumbling, wishing they had Miss

Simms, the last teacher, who never gave homework and spent most of the day singing songs to the kids. Some folks suspected it was because she could barely read and write, but the kids sure liked coming to school!

"And one other thing. We'll have spelling bees in class for the next three weeks. Everyone will have a chance to compete in the final one. First prize will be a five-dollar bill donated by Mr. Bentley, who was kind enough to send it in an envelope this morning to help the school."

"Five dollars!" the children exclaimed among themselves. That was more money than most of them had ever held in their lifetimes. Willy Bentley sat puffed up and proud over his father's donation.

"Why don't you just use it to buy everyone candy?" Terry asked. "That way we'd all be winners!"

"Let's go to my father's store now!" exclaimed Pierre Bedal.

"No, we'll not be spending this money on candy. This five-dollar bill is my reward to the one who studies hard and does well. Now, go out for recess, and don't make me angry. No fighting, spitting, or roughhousing. And if I hear any of you curse, I'll punish you severely."

She picked up a wooden paddle and hit her palm with it five times. "Now go!"

The kids bolted from their chairs and headed toward the playground. The Hardacre gang huddled at the door, staring at Terry.

Terry stuck his tongue out, wiggling like a monkey.

Miss O'Conner took it all in, knowing that playground justice was coming.

"That little rascal will be needin' the luck o' the Irish," she laughed to herself, wondering whether Terry had a touch of the Irish in him, with his red hair.

CHAPTER 12

THE INTERVIEW

Laura waited until the children had left, then walked up to the teacher. "Miss O'Conner, I'd like to introduce myself and tell you I'm sorry for disturbing your class."

Turning from the doorway, Maurene O'Conner smiled. "I know who you are, Mrs. Wilder. You're quite famous around here."

Blushing slightly, Laura went on. "Sometimes, I wish my name didn't have to appear in the newspaper."

Miss O'Conner walked to her desk and began straightening out papers. "What can I do for you, Mrs. Wilder? You don't have children in this school so you're here for another reason."

Laura laughed, "And I thought the Scotch were direct!"

"It's a trait I seemed to have picked up since coming to America."

"Oh, I think you had it before you got here," Laura

replied with a smile. "And why did you come, if I may ask?"

The teacher laughed. "Oh, come now, Mrs. Wilder, is that why you're here? To see what this Irish Catholic single woman is doing in the hills of Missouri?"

Laura sensed that things were getting off to a bad start. "No, Miss O'Conner, my editor thought the readers would find a story about the new teacher interesting. Your background is part of the story, but not the reason for the story."

"Editor, ah, now I see. His son Rudy Summers asked me who sent me here."

"He's just a boy. He doesn't know what he's saying," Laura said.

Miss O'Conner shook her head in disagreement. "Quite a big thought for a young lad to dream up." She smoothed her hair and looked straight at Laura. "You think by chance your employer has read any of that vile Klan literature I've found nailed on the school door?"

"Maybe. That's why a story on you is important. This would be an opportunity to let the community get to know you as a teacher."

Miss O'Conner laughed. "Mrs. Wilder, the Catholics and Protestants have been fighting for hundreds of years in Ireland, and they'll probably keep fighting hundreds more. The Klan's part of the same fight."

Miss O'Conner looked at Laura for a moment. "Just what is your article going to be about?" she asked.

Laura looked her in the eye. "I came here to do a story on you."

Miss O'Conner interrupted her. "Your article won't stop the hatred."

"It might help."

"Or it might hurt, depending on how it's written. Mrs. Wilder, I can't stop you from writing it, but I don't have to help you. I'd rather be left alone to teach. That's why I came to America."

"To be left alone, or to teach?"

"Both," the teacher said quietly.

Maurene thought about Michael McGuire lying dead in her arms and closed her eyes, trying to shut out the memory. Laura noticed.

Laura kept the interview going. "I'm glad to see that you believe in using the McGuffey readers and in strong discipline. Why, you've even got those Hardacres boys under control!"

A fire lit up behind Miss O'Conner's eyes. Laura had slipped, and she knew it immediately.

"And what's wrong with the Irish boys from the Hardacres? Just because their parents work the trees and farms of others doesn't mean they're born bad."

Laura stammered, "I didn't mean that I . . ."

Miss O'Conner interrupted her. "I know exactly what you mean. The children of the Hardacres get blamed for everything because they're Irish. 'If you can't blame anyone else, blame the Irish.' Isn't that the saying around here?"

"No," Laura said weakly.

Miss O'Conner erased the blackboard. "Since arriving here and living with the O'Reilly family, I've come to think that the children of the Hardacres are misunderstood angels."

Laura had lost control of the interview and knew it. "I've never heard them called that before."

"The people of this community would be better served if they worried more about books or a library than about the Hardacres children," Miss O'Conner said, dusting off the erasers.

"I'm glad to hear you say that, but . . ."

Miss O'Conner interrupted her again. ". . . but I can't understand you parents keeping your children home to work in the fields when they should be in school. Almost half the class didn't show up today. That's the height of stupidity!"

"I agree."

"You do?"

"Yes. Just because this is a rural community doesn't mean we're all stupid."

Now it was Miss O'Conner's turn to stammer. "I didn't mean that."

"Yes, you did. You think that anyone who lives on a farm is stupid and keeps their children out of school to work the fields. The problem is not unique to America. Why, I bet they have the same problem in Ireland."

Miss O'Conner backtracked. "Maybe, but my parents thought enough of me to send me to a private school and . . ."

"I send my daughter, Rose, to the best school in New Orleans."

"You do? Why? Isn't it expensive?"

A ball bounced against the outside school wall, shaking the pictures behind the teacher's desk.

Laura looked at Miss O'Conner. "I was never given the chance to go much beyond the fifth grade, and I wanted Rose to have the opportunities I didn't have. You've got a tough job teaching a group of mixed-aged students. I know, because I was a teacher."

Miss O'Conner sat down and lowered her defenses. "You were? I didn't know that."

"There's a lot you don't know about me or the people of this community. Just as you can't judge people by their accents, you can't judge people as inferior because they live on a farm."

Miss O'Conner noticed through the window that the students were gathering behind the schoolhouse. Something was up.

"Mrs. Wilder, write your article and tell them that this Irish lass has come to America to teach. Nothing else, just teach. And if you can correct their misimpressions of the lads of the Hardacres being rough cheats and liars, then you will have done everybody a service."

Laura put her pencil back in her purse. "I'll write the article as I see it, Miss O'Conner. Thank you for your time."

CHAPTER 13

CHOOSING SIDES

Behind the school, the children were gathered in a circle around Larry Youngun and Red Shaughnessy. Red had his fists up, but Larry had his hands down as he stood in front of his younger brother and Little James.

Laura heard the children shouting and stopped behind the trees near the schoolyard fence. She recognized Rev. Youngun's son Larry, who was up against one of the bigger Hardacres boys. She started to go break it up, but hesitated. She had already overstepped and interferred in the classroom.

Out of the corner of her eye she saw that Miss O'Conner was watching from the side window of the school building. Laura decided to wait and watch.

"Your brother's a wise-cracker, so move aside, Youngun!" Red Shaughnessy snarled, glaring at Larry.

Larry stood his ground. "You're twice his size, Red. Leave my brother and Little James alone."

Terry had his fingers crossed, hoping that Larry would scare them away.

Red stepped forward. "He's going to be taught a lesson, so move aside, or I'll teach you a lesson, too."

Gene Buchanan, Wiley O'Reilly, and the other boys from the Hardacres came up behind Red. They glared across the circle at Larry, who was all alone.

"Three against one's not fair!" shouted Johnny, leaning on his crutches.

"Shut up, crip," Gene growled, "or I'll burn your crutches."

Li and Frenchie came and stood beside Larry. Zeke stepped hesitantly beside them. Wiley spit on the ground and looked Frenchie in the eye.

"You're going against your religion, Frenchie. What do you want with them?"

Pierre didn't answer.

"Come on, Red," Gene sneered. "The minister's son got fancy, sissy shoes on. A regular pantywaist."

Some of the other kids who hadn't chosen sides looked at Larry's shoes and snickered.

A loud voice caught everyone off guard. "Don't be makin' fun of his shoes!" Missouri Poole pushed her way into the circle and shoved Red backward over the seesaw.

Red got up, dusting his pants off, "Gosh dangit, you ripped my pants!"

From under the schoolhouse, Dangit the dog rushed forward snarling. He bit into Red's pants leg and pulled him back over the seesaw again.

Laura stepped forward to break it up, but saw Miss O'Conner start down the steps. *What is she waiting for?* Laura asked herself.

Gene and Wiley rushed toward Larry. Li made a move and tripped Gene. Wiley grabbed Larry by the shirt.

Larry's shirt ripped wide open, and before Frenchie could stop him, Red hit Larry in the eye. Missouri Poole jumped into the fray and kicked Wiley in the shins.

Terry screamed, "Hit him, Larry. Hit him!"

Larry stood his ground, rubbing his eye, but not raising his fists. Red cocked his fist back again.

Finally, Miss O'Conner rushed forward. "Stop it! Stop it!" she shouted. "What is going on here?"

No one spoke. She looked at Larry's shirt. "Tell me, Mr. Youngun. What happened?"

The boys from the Hardacres glared at him. "Nothing," said Larry.

"He tried to pick a fight with me," Red said in his most innocent voice.

"Did you pick a fight with Red?"

"I didn't do nothing," Larry said, rubbing his eye.

Gene piped up. "We just wanted that squirt brother of his to quit makin' fun of us Irish Catholics and . . ."

Miss O'Conner put her hands on her hips and looked at Larry. "And why wouldn't you let your brother apologize? Or do you think it's right to make fun of Irish people?"

"No, no, that's not what happened!" Larry stammered. "They wanted to fight my brother and Little James and . . ."

Suddenly everyone seemed to be talking at once.

"Be quiet!" the teacher screamed. "Only one speak at a time!"

Red bowed his head. "We were just defending you, Miss O'Conner. We're proud to be Irish Catholics."

Laura waited for the teacher to lecture all the students. She was not expecting what the teacher said.

"That's all right, lads," she said, slipping back into her Irish brogue. She looked at Larry and the Youngun gang. "I will not tolerate this sort of behavior in my class. You are each going to write on the blackboard, 'I will not pick fights,' one hundred times."

"What about her?" Red asked, pointing to Missouri.

"Who?" Miss O'Conner asked.

"She was the worst of the bunch," said Gene.

"Gene, you are being rude. Apologize to this young lady."

Gene glared at Missouri. "Sorry . . . but you're no lady."

"That's not an apology," Larry said.

Laura stood on the edge of the grounds in complete agreement with Larry Youngun.

"Seems this is a case of the pot calling the kettle black, young man," Miss O'Conner said, looking at Larry. She turned to Missouri. "You come along too then, young lady. Now all of you march!"

Red tapped Larry and quietly said, "It ain't over yet,

preacher's son. I'm going to kick your behind all over the schoolyard. I'll make you fight."

Frenchie watched Gene walk off and turned to Larry. "Why didn't you hit him?"

Rubbing his eye, Larry looked down. "Pa said to turn the other cheek. Told me not to be fighting and to follow the Bible."

"Bible doesn't say anything about having to get wupped," Frenchie said.

"Quiet, you two," Miss O'Conner said, looking at Larry and Frenchie.

As the Youngun gang was marched toward the stairs, the Hardacres kids laughed and joked. Larry's eye was swelling shut. He was worried about what he'd tell his father.

"Turn the other cheek" had been drilled into him since birth. Larry had turned one and got hit in the eye. What was he to do now? Get two black eyes?

Terry and Little James decided to tag along, just to be on the safe side. They stood close to Larry, just out of reach of the Hardacres boys.

"We'll get you later," Red whispered to Terry.

Before Little James could stop him, Terry almost started the fight all over again, tossing air punches backed up by snarls. "Get this!" Terry said, sticking his tongue out and wiggling around. Red was so angry that his face matched the color of his flaming red hair.

With fists in the air, Red started toward Terry, but the teacher stopped him.

"Just remember, Red, sticks and stones will break

your bones but words will never hurt you." Miss O'Conner looked proud of herself for remembering an American saying.

Laura watched in shocked sadness. The Irish teacher was favoring the lying Hardacre boys. It was just what people wanted to hear. She could see the field day people would have with this information. It was true, yet it wasn't. Who was right and who was wrong? The children were just mimicking the hatreds of their homes, which always overshadows the good intentions of their churches.

Laura thought about what she'd seen and heard. There was more to it than the teacher favoring the Irish.

Old hatreds die hard. They seem to have a way of sticking their bony hands from the grave, infecting one generation after another, turning innocent children into name callers. When would it finally—if ever— end?

CHAPTER 14

WE'RE WATCHING YOU

Summers heard the bell tinkle over the door. Wiping the ink from his hands onto his apron, he went into the newspaper's front office.

Three men stood there. They were strangers to Summers, although perhaps he had seen them over in the next county.

"Good to see you, Summers," said the dark-haired stranger.

Summers peered at the man. "Do I know you, stranger?"

"Well, we ain't never spoke before, but I've been sending you my thoughts."

Summers laughed. "Well, a lot of people think about what I write. Is there anything special you want?"

The dark-haired stranger took off his hat and dusted it against his dungarees. "We just want to know when you're goin' to be printin' the words of the Dragon."

"The dragon?" Summers asked wearily.

The short, stocky one stepped forward. "He's talkin' 'bout the letters from the Grand Dragon of the Ozarks."

"I know you've been gettin' them," said the dark-haired man, " 'cause Jefferson here has been slipping them under your door."

The tall skinny man shook his head up and down, trying to hold back his naturally stupid-faced grin. "Yup, I've been puttin' 'em under the door like I was told to."

Suddenly it dawned on Summers. They were talking about the Klan letters he'd been receiving, the ones he had mentioned to Laura.

"Oh, those letters," Summers replied. "I wondered who was sending them."

The dark-haired man came up to Summers and poked him in the belly. "We just want you to know that we're watching you. We want you to print the truth about the new teacher."

"I've got my best reporter working on a story about the new teacher at this moment."

The three men smiled. "Good," said the dark-haired man. "The people of this county need to be warned. They've got to be told the truth."

Summers just wanted them to go. "Gentlemen, I appreciate your stoppin' by. I'm sure you'll be quite surprised by the story that Laura Ingalls Wilder writes."

The stocky one opened the door and the tall, skinny one stepped out. The dark-haired leader turned to leave, then stopped and looked at Summers. "We'll be watching for it, and we'll be watchin' you."

Summers stood there as the tinkling bell echoed their departure.

CHAPTER 15

BURGOO

As the Younguns, Li, Little James, and Missouri Poole picked up their books to leave the schoolhouse, Sweet sat on the steps, working on his tenth doughnut. Terry came out first and grabbed the last bite from Sweet's fat fingers.

"Hey, no fair, that was mine!" yelled Sweet as Terry popped the piece of doughnut into his mouth.

Zeke said, "With your eyes closed, you look like a hippo being fed."

"What's a hippo?" asked Sherry.

"It's goin' to be a long school year," moaned Frenchie as the Youngun gang headed down the dirt road.

"Think we all should move in with Janson Leidenburg. That lucky cuss don't have to go to school," Terry said.

"Durn Catholics." Missouri looked at Frenchie. "Sorry, Frenchie, forgot you were one."

She pulled out her pipe and lit it up. "Want a puff?" she asked Larry, who just shook his head no.

"It ain't the Catholics' fault," Frenchie said. "My dad says the Hardacres are troublemakers 'cause they're poor."

"I wish they'd all move somewhere else," Little James said.

"Wouldn't you miss Red Shaughnessy?" Larry kidded.

Little James stuck his finger in the air. "If you wants to see how much I'd miss 'em, just stick your finger in the creek and pull it out and look at the hole."

"What hole?" Zeke asked.

"That's just it. There ain't no hole and we ain't goin' to miss 'em if he moved away."

"Wish they'd go and move with their own kind," said Li. Little James agreed and Frenchie seconded it.

The black boy, Chinese boy, and the French-Canadian boy all agreed that the Irish boys should move away. Their parents, who had all been victims of prejudice during their lives, seemed to have forgotten to mention that fact to their children.

"You all want to come to my house to eat?" Little James asked.

"Who's doin' the cookin'? You?" Li laughed.

"Naw, my sisters, Ruby, Pearl, and Opal, are goin' to wup up some 'Filthy McNasty.' It's good!"

" 'Filthy McNasty'? What's that?" Zeke asked.

"Zeke, don't you know nothin'? Filthy McNasty is

what you call burgoo." Zeke was still bewildered. "Burgoo boy, take that beanie off and put some brains in your head."

"You havin' a burgoo party?" Terry asked.

Little James pulled up his belt loops proudly. "We're goin' to celebrate the baptizin' of my cousin."

"Your cousin Baby Venus?" asked Larry, rubbing his shiner.

"Naw," said Little James. "It's the baptizin' of my cousin Angel May Ruth Lee Mary Jane Lethadorie."

Frenchie interrupted him. "With a name that long, you're goin' to need a lot of water for the baptizin'!"

Missouri leaned forward and planted a kiss on Larry's cheek which he quickly rubbed off. She blew a smoke ring toward him with an air kiss inside.

"That pipe smells something awful!" said Larry.

Missouri took a deep drag on the pipe and blew another smoke ring toward him. "It's my pa's special blend. I think it smells just like cookies in the oven." She blew another smoke ring toward him.

Larry twitched his nose at the smell. "I think it smells more like meadow muffins in the field."

They all laughed and poked at Little James who danced around. "I still don't know what burgoo is," said Zeke. "I don't know if I can eat it."

Little James was puzzled. "It's got chickens, ducks, corn, turnips, collards, potatoes, peppers, possum, and spices. Can you eat that?"

"I guess so," Zeke said, adjusting his skullcap.

"What were you worried about?" Missouri asked.

"Pork meat," Zeke replied.

Little James slapped Zeke on the back. "If you're worrying 'bout not having enough pork meat to eat, well, that's no problem. My sister Ruby puts in all the pork meat and scraps she can find. You'll get your fill!"

Little James didn't see the sour face Zeke made.

Little James put his arm around Zeke's shoulder and continued. "Yes sir, Ruby puts in pig's feet, pig's brains, and bacon and drippin's and cracklin's and hocks and some pig's tail, snout, and—oh, yes,—pig's eyeballs, and hot buttered chitlins!" Little James stood on his heels proudly.

Little James didn't know that Jews weren't supposed to eat pork, and by the time he had finished, Zeke decided to head home and eat kosher!

Sherry had no problem eating burgoo. As a matter of fact, she was already smacking her lips. "Can I say the blessin'?" she asked, taking the thumb from her mouth.

"No!" said Larry and Terry simultaneously.

As everyone except Zeke headed toward Little James's house for a snack, a wagon load of farm kids who didn't go to school passed them by.

"Life would be sweet if we didn't have to go to school," said Frenchie.

"Who needs school, anyway?" asked Missouri.

"Need this!" Terry called, wiggling around and racing up the dirt road.

The Youngun gang went racing after him, taking the shortcut. They saw Laura walking on the road below them as they crossed Devil's Ridge.

CHAPTER 16

CAUSIN' TROUBLE

The three Klan members looked down from the hill at the schoolhouse. Laura was leaving, and a few kids were playing in the field behind the school.

"How long you want to wait up here?" the thin man asked.

"I was hopin' she'd leave and go back to the Hardacres," the Klan leader grumbled. "Then we could break the windows and mess up her desk."

"I still don't understand," said the stocky man. "Why would the Irish want to mess up her desk?"

"That's the point," the Grand Dragon smiled. "We'll go down to the saloon and spread it around that the Irish are causin' trouble. Even messed up the Irish teacher's desk, they did."

"They did?" the stocky man asked, scratching his head.

"No, they didn't! I'm just tellin' you what the others will believe if we tell 'em the Irish did it."

After thirty minutes, the boss stood up. "Come on,

let's go. I guess she ain't leavin' the school any time too soon."

"Where we gonna go?" asked the thin man.

"Let's go check out the Hardacres."

"I don't want to fight," the stocky man whined.

"I'm not talkin' 'bout fightin'," the Klan leader snapped.

They took the back paths across the ridges and through the ravines. As they neared Hardacre Hill, they crept along, hidden by the bushes, so the loggers riding the timber wagons wouldn't see them.

Children were playing tag in the dusty road that ran between the small cabins and shanties. Several women were gossiping near the water pump, and a group of men were talking with Father Walsh, the local priest.

The thin man looked over the log and then back at the boss. "We can't do nothin' with all those people down there."

"I'll think of somethin'," the Klan leader said.

The church bells rang out from the Catholic church, and the women and men joined Father Walsh.

"Where they goin'?" the stocky man asked.

"How do I know?" the Klan leader asked, then snapped his fingers. "I've got it!"

"What?" the two men asked.

"Give me one of the handbills," the Grand Dragon said. "Be quick about it."

The stocky man nervously pulled one from his coat pocket, and the boss began scribbling with his pen. "This ought to stir things up," he smiled.

"What's it say?" the thin man asked.

"When are you goin' to learn to read?" the Dragon snapped.

"Don't need to read to shoe horses," the man shrugged.

The Grand Dragon showed them what he'd written and read it. "It says, 'Irish go home . . . and take your teacher with you. We're watchin' you.' "

"Who's watchin'?" the thin man asked.

"We're watchin' . . . that's why I signed it 'Grand Dragon of the KKK.' " He handed it to the thin man.

"What you want me to do with it?"

"Go post it on that pole by the water pump."

"But what if someone sees me?" the thin man asked.

"There are so many Irish always comin' and goin' in the Hardacres that they'll just think you're one of them," the Dragon laughed.

"They'll think I'm a Catholic? Do I look like one?"

The stocky man looked over the log and back at his friend. "You do sort of look like one," he nodded.

"What?" the thin man stammered, looking over the log at the people of the Hardacres heading to church.

The Grand Dragon stood up and pulled the thin man to his feet. "Catholics look like anybody else, that's what's so bad."

"Yeah, you can't tell them from us," the stocky man said, shaking his head. "It's a lot easier stirrin' up trouble between blacks and whites."

"Get on down there and put that up. We've got to send another message."

"To who, boss?" the thin man asked.

"To that newspaper editor. I think if we scare him enough, he'll write stories that will do all our recruitin' for us."

CHAPTER 17

THE SQUIRREL'S PAW

The three Younguns were huddled in the dining room. Larry and Terry wanted Sherry to agree not to tell Pa what had happened on the playground.

"Do you understand, squirt?" Terry said.

"Promise, cross my heart, and hope to fly," said Sherry.

"The word's *die,* you dummy," Terry said, jostling her.

"Quiet! Here comes Pa," Larry whispered. Rev. Youngun came marching down the hall, Bible in hand. "Uh-oh, it's goin' to be a Good Book lecture."

"Cover your eye. Tell him the light bothers you," whispered Terry.

Their father's voice boomed out, "I told you children to come right home after school! Did you stop and swim after I told you all not to?"

"No, Pa," they all answered in unison.

Rev. Youngun was an imposing figure in the doorway, with his black suit, Sunday-shined shoes, Bible in hand, and something mysterious wrapped in newspaper.

He'd had to help at a funeral over in the next county and minister to an old woman over in the south hollow. He was in no mood for Youngun shenanigans.

Rev. Youngun stood and stared at his three children. Their eyes were looking anywhere and everywhere except at him. He wondered why Larry had his hand over one eye.

"What's wrong with your eye?"

"Nothing, Pa. Just got an itch."

From under the table came a loud burp.

"What was that?" Rev. Youngun asked, lifting up the tablecloth.

Dangit the dog was laying on his back, feet straight up in the air. He let loose another loud belch and a small stream of tiny dog flatulence.

"I think that dog has eaten something bad," Rev. Youngun said as Dangit burped again.

"Not bad—good, Pa," Terry said shyly.

"Why is it good that Dangit has eaten something bad?" he asked his auburn-haired son.

"No, Pa," Larry said. "What Terry's tryin' to say is that Dangit feels bad 'cause he ate somethin' good."

"Yeah, Pa," chirped Sherry. "Dangit ate too much Ruby burgoo."

"Ruby burgoo? What's that, bug droppings?" Rev. Youngun asked, getting sick to his stomach at the thought.

"It's just Filthy McNasty, Pa," answered Larry, telling Pa the other hill name for burgoo.

"Bug droppings and bat droppings can make you sick," his father said. "You knew that Dangit was eating Ruby burgoo, and you didn't stop him?"

Larry shrugged his shoulders, not knowing what to say.

"I ate some too, Pa," Sherry said proudly.

"I licked it off my fingers!" said Terry.

Images of his children on their hands and knees eating an enormous pile of burgoo appalled him. *They really need a mother to watch out for them,* he thought. If people in the church heard that his children had been eating bug droppings while he was ministering, it would be the talk of the town and the death of his reputation.

He could hear it now. "Yeah, there goes the minister whose kids eat bug poop. Made a meal out of a ruby burgoo. Why listen to him when he can't even take care of his own kids?"

"You'd like to eat some of Ruby's burgoo, Pa. It'd stick to your tongue and lips like burgoo never did before."

He almost retched! "Stop it! Stop it! Why were you eating bug droppings?"

The three Youngun kids looked at each other and laughed.

"Not bug droppings, Pa," Larry exclaimed, holding his hand over his eye. "Little James's sister Ruby made up a mess of burgoo that we had for our second lunch."

Rev. Youngun was relatively wise to the world for a man of the cloth, but he'd never eaten or heard of burgoo. So they told him all about Ruby, Pearl, and Opal's burgoo and how Dangit had gotten up on a chair when no one was looking and eaten his fill.

Terry laughed, "If he'd slipped in the pot, Ruby said she'd have just cooked him right along with the rest of it!"

Rev. Youngun tried to change the subject to something he understood. "What did you children do today in school? Sherry?"

"I played on the playground and drew pictures and ate my lunch and . . . and . . ."

"Yes? Anything else?"

Sherry thought for a moment, then brightened up, "And I went to the outhouse by myself."

"Went fishing for brains," Terry whispered.

"What did you say, son?" his father asked politely.

"Nothing," Terry said, fiddling with his collar. "I was just wishing for rain. I like the sound of it on the old tin roof when I'm sleeping. Reminds me of the nights when Ma used to sing me to sleep."

Terry had a way of starting out kidding and ending up thinking of Ma and getting himself so worked up that he would cry. Which is what he did now. Sherry saw him crying and grabbed up her blanket and dolly and began crying.

"I miss Momma," Sherry blubbered.

Rev. Youngun could feel the situation slipping from

his grasp. He picked up Sherry and smoothed Terry's hair.

"Now, now, children, it will be all right. I miss your mother too." It finally dawned on him that Larry had been covering his eye the whole time. "Why are you covering your eye?"

"Just feel like it, Pa," Larry said.

"Gots a shiner!" whispered Sherry. "He got hit in the playground fight with Red Shaughnessy."

Rev. Youngun's eyes went wide. "A fight! You know I don't approve of fighting of any kind."

Larry dropped his hand from his swollen eye. It was almost swollen shut. "Pa, I didn't fight. I was . . ."

His father interrupted him. "And didn't I tell you that the Bible says, 'A soft answer turneth away wrath: but grievous words stir up anger'?"

Larry looked down. "Pa, I didn't fight Red Shaughnessy. He hit me. I turned the other cheek like you said, but I don't want to . . ."

"What don't you want, son?"

Larry raised his head and looked his father in the eye. "I don't want to have to love him. I'm so mad at him that I'm thinkin' thoughts I shouldn't be thinkin'."

"I know it's hard not to fight when someone takes a punch at you, but I want you to turn the other cheek," Rev. Youngun said, examining Larry's eye.

"That's easier said than done. Ouch!" Larry winced as his father's fingers hit a tender spot on his face.

Rev. Youngun looked at the swollen eye and felt compassion for his son. "We'll talk about it later. Let's get some ice on this before it gets any worse."

Rev. Youngun walked Larry into the kitchen. As he took a chunk of ice to the table to break into smaller pieces, he looked again at Larry's eye.

"He tagged you a good one, didn't he, son?"

"Red hit me good, Pa," Larry said.

"Here," Rev. Youngun said, wrapping the broken ice in a towel, "hold this against your eye."

"What's in the newspaper, Pa?" Terry asked, looking at the package on the counter.

"Dr. George got them as payment for a bill from some poor hill folk and thought we'd like to have them." He unwrapped the newspapers and held up four squirrels. "Think you all can eat some squirrel, or did you eat too much of Ruby's burgoo?" he laughed.

The Youngun kids loved squirrel. Those scrawny looking things tasted like possum combined with venison.

"I get the brains!" Larry screamed out.

"No, Pa, he got the brains last time!" Terry said, stamping his feet.

"Some people would question whether either of you have ever gotten any brains, but we'll let that go for now." Rev. Youngun was quite pleased with his inside joke. "You kids clean them up and we'll have a fine dinner of fricasseed squirrel with mushroom catsup and the carrot pudding and rich cakes that Mrs. Springer brought over this morning."

Terry picked up one of the squirrels and held it in front of Sherry's face. "You get to eat the tail—raw."

"Pa!" she screamed. "I don't want the tail!"

Terry chased her around the room, holding the squirrel with feet outstretched. "Flyin' squirrel's goin' to get you," he screamed as he raced around the room.

Rev. Youngun caught him by the seat of his pants. "Stop that kind of talk! Terry, it's your turn to clean the squirrels. Larry will cook 'em, cause he's the only one who knows how your ma used to make 'em. Sherry, you set the table."

Eating squirrel was like eating rabbit and duck for pioneer Americans. When the early immigrants stepped onto Plymouth Rock, they were not prepared for new-world cuisine. If the Indians hadn't taught them how to survive and learn to live off the abundance in the woods, they would have never lived to have the Boston Tea Party. Rabbits and squirrels were running loose everywhere. So they became very popular main dishes, although they were such scrawny critters.

Terry cut and skinned the critters. Their ma had been quite a cook, and Larry had grown up with her in the kitchen. He was the only one who could decipher her recipe notes. He cooked the first batch and put them on a platter in front of Terry, who was fooling around at the table.

Terry *was* up to something, which was not unusual. As a matter of fact, he could be up to nothing and have it end up something. He was fooling with the cooked squirrels on the table, tying and cutting something with his pocketknife.

With the table set and everyone in their places, Rev. Youngun began: "Father, we thank You for Your blessings and the . . ."

While Pa closed his eyes and said the blessing, his children peeked around the room.

". . . and the guidance You've given us. We lift up our hands . . ."

Terry pulled on a piece of fishing line that he'd tied onto one of the largest squirrel's paws. He slowly raised the paw and waved it at Sherry.

Rev. Youngun was oblivious to all as he continued with the blessing. ". . . up our hands and say . . ." He was right in the middle when Sherry stood up on her chair and screamed.

Rev. Youngun stopped in midsentence and looked at her. "What's the matter, Sherry?"

"The squirrel waved at me, Pa! It's still alive!"

Rev. Youngun sighed. "No, it's not, Sherry. Be still."

Terry sat there with head bowed and eyes closed, holding back a grin as Sherry sat down.

Rev. Youngun bowed his head and closed his eyes. "Let me continue. Lord, we lift up our hands and know that Your path is the true way. We ask You to ask all Your servants to lift up their hands and . . ."

Terry now raised both of the squirrel's paws and waggled them at Sherry.

Sherry gasped loudly.

Rev. Youngun stopped again. He looked at wide-eyed

Sherry, one-eyed Larry, and closed-eyed Terry. Something wasn't right. "Terry, are you doing something?"

"Me, Pa?" Terry asked, shrugging his shoulders.

"Look at his paws!" Sherry exclaimed, pointing to the fricasseed squirrel's paws. She reached out and touched one hesitantly, then sat down.

Terry looked at his sister and reached toward the squirrel he'd rigged up, using his conversation as a cover while he undid the fishing line. "She's crazy, Pa. Next thing you know she'll be sayin' the milk glass moos."

Rev. Youngun saw through the subterfuge and caught Terry's hand. "Well, well, what have we here?"

He took the fishing line from Terry's hand and pulled on the squirrel's paws. They went up and down.

"Sorry, Pa," Terry said with downcast eyes. "Just playin' a joke on Sherry, that's all."

Rev. Youngun knew he had to punish him, but inside he was amused at the ingeniousness of his auburn-haired son. "What do you have to say for yourself?"

From under the table, Dangit let a long belch. They all burst out laughing.

"Sorry, Pa," Terry said, trying not to smile.

"If you can remember any of the proverbs I've tried to teach you, then I will accept your apology. Otherwise, you'll do the dishes by yourself."

Terry closed his eyes and scratched his head. He looked at the ceiling, at his brother, down at Dangit. Nothing came to him.

"Terry, just try to remember. I won't rebuke you if you get it wrong."

Suddenly it came to Terry! " 'A wise son heareth his father's instruction: but a scorner heareth not rebuke.' "

Rev. Youngun never knew how the auburn-haired moptop did it, but he did it. "Amen," he said. "Now let's eat."

"I want some brains, Pa," Larry and Terry cried out together.

"So do I," Rev. Youngun mumbled. "So do I."

CHAPTER 18

THE MESSAGE

Summers was busy putting the day's newspaper to bed. He pondered running the story he heard about Silvia Leidenburg being beaten by her drunken husband, but he didn't want to add to the family's pain.

As the street lamps glowed on the streets of Mansfield, he closed the office door to keep out the noise from Tippy's Saloon three doors down.

The mail had been piling up in the office for several days. Since most of the mail was bills, it just seemed easier to let it pile up until money came in or he was in a mood for punishment.

While putting the bills into three stacks of pay, put off, and forget about for now, he came across a folded piece of paper. Summers sat back in his chair, loosened his tie, and read the letter:

Dear misser Summer.
We r watchin' what u print in yur paper. The Klan is everywear.

We r powerful. Support the KKK and it's fight.
Schools should bee taught bi Americans.
Gran Dragon of the Ozarks

"I've gotten myself in a box now," he said to the stuffed razorback hog in the corner. A tapping at the window made him jump. It was Sheriff Sven Peterson.

"Everything all right, Andrew?" the sheriff asked, poking his head in the door.

"Just the usual, Sheriff. Couple of bills and crank letters in the mail," Summers fibbed.

"Means someone is at least reading what you print," the sheriff laughed. "You should be happy for that."

As the sheriff waved good-bye and closed the door, Summers looked at the Klan letter again.

Someone was reading his paper all right, he thought to himself. The wrong someone!

CHAPTER 19

CLASSED AS ILLITERATES

Laura worked all evening on the article for the *Mansfield Monitor,* deciding to ignore the issue of Miss O'Conner favoring the Irish children and instead spotlight the issue of farm children not going to school. She left the article on the kitchen counter for Manly to read in the morning.

She drifted off to a troubled sleep, with visions of children slaving in the fields, with no future except to follow in the footsteps of their parents, unable to read the signposts of life.

Manly got up in the night to get a glass of milk. His stomach was growling, so he made himself a country ham sandwich with sliced onions, tomatoes, and lots of mustard.

In the back of the icebox he found some greens and a hard-boiled egg, so he added that until the sandwich was almost three inches thick!

He sat down at the kitchen table and took a big bite. As the mustard dripped down his chin, he reached for a towel to wipe it off. He picked up Laura's article by mistake and almost wiped his face with it. Turning up the light, Manly sat back and began to read as the mustard dried on his chin.

CLASSED AS ILLITERATES
By Laura Ingalls Wilder

Among all the beautiful sights and sounds of Fall and harvest time, there is an ugly blot on the landscape. It shows as little promise for the future as a blighted fruit tree. It is the presence of children at work in the fields when they should be in school.

As I was walking to interview the new Mansfield schoolteacher, I saw dozens of children who should have been in school. Many of them had never even been inside a classroom because their parents don't think that reading and writing are very important.

Is it because they can't read themselves and want to perpetuate their own ignorance? Is that why they had children? To prove to the world that illiteracy isn't so bad, that the ignorant can get by without books, without knowing how to read and write, that ignorance in vast numbers is all right?

I think it is a disgrace! We have a new teacher. Her name is Maurene O'Conner, and yes, she is an Irish Catholic. But her being Catholic is the least of your worries.

What you should be worried about is allowing children to miss school to work the farms. If you are only having children to raise farmhands, like breeding cattle, then all you wives and farmers should get out of bed and put "help wanted" ads in this paper.

There is a state law that children have to go to school. It has gone unobserved because it is convenient to do so.

I say we must enforce the law and that every child must be brought to school each morning—even if it means that the sheriff has to fine or arrest all the parents of the truants. Maybe that is the only way we can stop this breeding of ignorance!

If you think that we cannot afford to give children proper schooling because their help is needed on the farm, then think again! We shall pay for the education that we do not give them. Oh, yes, we will pay!

We will have another generation of inefficient and educationally handicapped children, held back and suffering for the lack of knowledge denied them because they were needed on the farm.

Just like saying your ABC's, the decision is yours. Don't deny your children an education—send them to school.

He read it again, sipping the cold milk slowly. Manly put the article down and took another bite of sandwich.

"Summers ain't goin' to like this," he said to himself, chewing on a juicy slice of onion, "and neither will most of the town."

At breakfast the next morning, Laura made fluffy sour-cream pancakes with Ozark sausage treats and baking powder biscuits. The secret to the pancakes was adding sour cream and beaten egg whites to the batter.

As the pancakes bubbled on the griddle, Laura took from the oven the Ozark sausage treats. The bottom of the casserole was lined with sliced potatoes and the top was a layer of sausage covered with sliced apples from their own orchard.

Her biscuits were made with lard and cut into rounds. They were perfect with some of the reheated red-eye gravy from the other morning.

After breakfast Manly helped clear the table. "That article is pretty strong, Laura," he said, putting a plate on the shelf.

"It's the truth," she answered, putting the rest of the sausage treats into the icebox.

"What's Summers going to say?" he asked her.

Laura laughed. "He told me to check out the school, and I did. But he should have told me to check out the fields. That's where most of the kids are!"

"Summers ain't goin' to like it one bit," Manly said, wiping out a coffee cup.

"If he doesn't like it, then he can just print that crazy Klan literature. No one in town would ever read his paper again," she said.

"Things at the bottom of the pond ain't always like the surface," Manly said to his wife. "What's under the lily pad is not always a frog; sometimes it's a snake."

The phone rang and Manly picked up the receiver. "This is Manly Wilder. Who's callin'?"

"This is Summers. Did she write the article?"

Manly watched Laura wrap the leftover biscuits. "Oh, she wrote you an article, she did."

Summers was relieved. "Good. I'll leave a hole for it on the front page. When will I get it?"

"I'll bring it to town in about an hour."

Summers was satisfied, so after the kitchen was cleaned up, Manly took Laura's article to the newspaper office.

Summers didn't read the article until Laura dropped by in the late afternoon to see what he thought about it. He opened the envelope and read "Classed as Illiterates" while she stood watching.

As he read, his eyes went from wide to wider. This was not going to please his visitors or most of the farmers in the county.

Summers took off his glasses and rubbed his eyes. "This article is going to bring the town down around our ears!"

"It's all true," Laura said, putting away her writing tablet.

"Maybe so, but there ain't no way that the harvest can be brought in without keeping the kids out of school. It would ruin the economy 'round here, and that ain't the American way."

"Scoundrels wrap themselves in Old Glory when they run up against truth. The law says that these kids are to be in school, and I think it should be enforced!"

"I asked you to write about the new teacher, and all you gave me in this article is a paragraph on her."

"I said I'd write something about her, and I did," Laura said coyly.

"Well, you slipped one by me this time, you did. Makin' fun of what I asked you to investigate. Did you even look around a little while you were there?"

"Andrew Jackson Summers, I wrote the story as I saw it . . . just as you said I could."

Summers snorted. "Why'd you become a writer, anyway? Who asked you to write for this paper in the first place?"

Laura laughed. "You asked me to write for the paper last year, or have you forgotten?"

"But why are you always so fired up about some things you write about? Can't you write about women's things like cookin' and cleanin'?"

Laura just shook her head. "I would have loved to have been a doctor or elected to Congress, but since women can't even vote, there's not much chance of that for me. But God gave me the gift of writing, which gives me the chance to change the wrongs I see around me."

Summers pushed a plate of half-eaten food to the edge of his desk, to make room for the newspaper layout. "You're a dreamer, Laura, a real dreamer."

"Andrew, if I see things that are wrong and just turn and walk away, then I've condoned those wrongs. I can't do that, no matter how uncomfortable it makes you to publish what I write. Fire me if you don't like what I do, but don't ask me to stop speaking my mind."

Summers waved his arms in dismay. "Go on. Get on

back to Apple Hill Farm and figure out other ways to make my life miserable. Don't know why I pay you to write and give me a headache!"

"Good-bye, Andrew," Laura said, pausing by the front door.

Summers picked up the article. "If I had more time, I'd write it myself, but I saved a hole on the front page for your article." He began walking toward the back room. "Dag-gone-it, I'm going to lose my bet."

"What bet?" she asked.

"I bet the boys at Tippy's that you'd come back with a humdinger of an article on the teacher. You came up with a humdinger, all right. You humdinged me out of five bucks!"

"Everyone will like it," she laughed, walking out the door.

"Not everyone," Summers said, knowing that what he was about to print would bring trouble to his door.

During dinner that evening, Laura did most of the talking, relating over and over every moment of her meeting with Summers. Laura was excited and didn't notice Manly's growing irritation. She didn't even ask his opinion.

Manly set his hat down. "Laura, my parents kept me home to do farmwork, and your parents kept you home because school was not all that important. What's so danged important about getting everyone so riled up?"

Laura stared at her husband. "Manly Wilder, just because we're home-taught doesn't mean everyone should be. We had parents who knew how to read and write, but how can kids be home-taught by parents who can't read or write?"

Manly saw the fire in Laura's eyes. She was off on another crusade, and there was nothing he could do about it except go along or get out of the way.

"Laura, maybe it's just that I don't want to have to be duckin' and worryin' 'bout who agrees with who at the feed store in town. I just want to live and let live. We got good times now, girl."

Laura softened. She knew that each time she took hold of an issue, Manly suffered. When she took it upon herself to save the trees around Mansfield, it nearly tore the town apart. Manly had been caught in the middle and ended up getting roughed up and threatened.

Manly looked at her. "I know you're thinkin' that all's well that ends well, but how do you know how this will end? We're lucky 'cause we can hire men to work our crops and orchards."

"If we can do it, they can do it," she said, crossing her arms.

Manly shuffled his feet. "Well, you know that ain't necessarily so. It's easy to preach, but it ain't never easy to be the worker bee."

"But if the worker bees are too ignorant to read the signs pointing to the nest, then they'll be working at nothing."

"Not everyone's like you, Laura."

She caught hold of her emotions and looked at her husband. "I think I'm going to count to ten and say I love you."

Her article was a humdinger, all right. By the afternoon it was the talk of the town, and Summers had a note slipped under his door:

U LIED!
THEE GRAN DRAGON IS WATCHING U!

Freedom of the press carries with it a heavier burden than I ever imagined, Summers thought.

CHAPTER 20

ANOTHER HUMDINGER!

Laura's next article was another humdinger! Summers almost had a fit and only ran it because he was short on time.

He knew it would cause more trouble, but since sales were up, he'd grin and bear it. And he secretly felt there was some truth to what Laura was saying.

He read Laura's latest article again. "If it weren't for that Irish teacher, I'd be out wavin' the flag with her!" he said after finishing it.

Having heard nothing from the Klan in several days, Summers just hoped for the best as he prepared to have the type set.

WE CARE MORE FOR HORSES THAN
CHILDREN
By Laura Ingalls Wilder
How many of you have spent hundreds of dollars on your horses? Breeding and training them to develop the best of the breed costs money, a lot of

money. I've heard the men and women of the community brag that horses are the most important things in their lives.

I guess what it really boils down to is that we as a community care more for training horses than training and educating our own children. Compare how much we spend on animals to how much we as a community spend on education, and I think you'll agree that it's disgraceful!

I've heard that a lot of people were upset over my column about enforcing the law and keeping children in school.

Yes, keeping them home will force some farmers to either work longer hours or spend some money to hire extra help. Children should not be brought into this world just to be farmhands. Raising children and teaching them to run a farm and appreciating the land is proper. Raising children to be field hands is not.

Why, as a community, do we treat education as lower than fixing the Willow Creek Bridge? Remember when some of the rails broke last year? Why, a day hardly went by before there were a dozen men from the community sawing and hammering and putting it all back together.

But what about fixing our local educational outlook or repairing the school? What you should be worried about is that we as a community only give enough money to have one teacher for over thirty children of mixed ages. We say education is important but won't spend the money to improve "the old red school house" that so many of you claim to hold dear.

"It leaked in my time," an old farmer told me, "so they can get by too."

But if someone told that farmer that he'd have to plow his fields with a broken plow, he'd raise such cane that the whole county would hear him.

Well, I say that a classroom without enough books or proper heating and a leaking roof is just as bad. No, it is worse!

I say that we need to petition Sheriff Peterson to bring in the kids who aren't in school and fine the parents and arrest them if necessary. For they are not just hurting themselves, they are hurting the future of our town, our state, and our nation.

If you agree, then make sure you send your children to school and encourage others to do so. Ring the bell for educating our young people!

By the end of the week, farmers were complaining that Summers was trying to destroy the economy of the town. A load of manure was mysteriously dumped on the paper's front steps, and there was talk of petitioning the state for a law making school optional for farm children.

The town was choosing sides.

Laura began speaking to church groups and the county ladies' clubs. The fire was in her soul on this issue, and she was like a dog with a bone who wouldn't let go.

Manly felt like a sitting duck when he went to the feed store that afternoon. Though it was a relatively warm afternoon, there was a frost in the store. It was filled with farmers, and none of them wanted to talk to the "traitor's husband," as he had been called by an old farmer on the outskirts of town.

For Manly, Apple Hill Farm became his safe haven. No one at the feed store wanted to chew the fat with him without arguing about Laura's articles, and most of the other farmers didn't want anything much to do with him at all!

"For better or for worse," he said as Laura left for another speech in the next county.

One thing that Manly always liked to do was eat. Big eating had been part of his life since growing up on the farm in upstate New York. As long as he was eating something, everything didn't seem so bad.

There was a little nip in the air, so Manly decided to make up a pot of Ozark chili. He opened up the icebox door and took out whatever he felt like . . . beef, country ham, and some mustard. He sliced and diced all the meat together and heated it in the pan with some butter.

Once it was browned, he added two cans of red kidney beans, a handful of paprika, two handfuls of chili powder and salt, cayenne pepper, and five bay leaves. After an hour of simmering, he crushed in crackers and hunks of cheese that he'd found in the back of the icebox and topped it with a half-inch of fresh-cut onions.

As he ate the chili, savoring each bite, he began feeling a bit guilty. Laura was out speaking about what she believed in and organizing the women of the town. But what was he doing?

Manly was not the type to seek out confrontations, which was why he had been putting off getting the supplies he needed from the feed store. If he didn't do something, then wasn't he in effect giving silent support to those opposed to his wife's views?

Wrestling with the issue was harder than eating the last of the Ozark chili, but it gave him time to make up his mind. He liked that old saying that "actions speak louder than words."

Manly thought doing something was just as important—maybe more important—than talking about doing something. So without telling anyone, not even Laura, he began spending his time in the late afternoons repairing the things at school Laura had written about.

Laura was too busy going around and speaking to notice what he was up to. She just assumed he was hanging out or playing checkers in town when his work was done.

Manly went over to the school and made a list of what needed to be done, and then began doing it. Over the course of several trips he had been able to scrub and weatherproof the stairs after replacing two boards. He painted the inside walls with the extra paint from his attic and removed the black heel marks on the base-boards with steel wool dampened with mineral spirits. After that he waxed them bright.

The teacher's chair needed fixing, so he brought wood glue on his next visit and then sanded and cedar oiled the coatroom. Manly almost coughed to death trying to clean out the stovepipe and even Miss O'Conner laughed when he ended up looking like a raccoon!

The hardest project that awaited him was to repair the roof. Replace would be more accurate. There were so many holes and weak spots that Manly doubted the roof would make it through the winter.

The thought of children sitting under a potential disaster appalled him. It was just something that had to be done, so he would do it alone, if necessary.

The only one who knew what Manly was up to was Miss O'Conner, who let him hammer and saw away after she locked the school door for the evening. He had politely told her what he wanted to do and didn't give a reason for it.

Since his wife was writing the articles, Miss O'Conner thought that everyone knew what Manly was up to, but that no one had heeded Laura's calls to fix up the schoolhouse.

No one except Manly.

"America is a strange place," Miss O'Conner said to herself as she walked back to the Hardacres.

CHAPTER 21

DADDY, PLEASE COME HOME

For a few days, Thomas Leidenburg straightened up. Swore he'd never drink again; that he'd "go on the wagon" and change his life.

The first evening, Thomas Leidenburg was helpful around the house, but nervous as a cat. His body was craving alcohol and no matter how hard he tried to control it, his temper was short. On the second day, as he worked the orchards with Janson and Sil, all he could think about was a drink.

That afternoon, he took all the money and headed into town, leaving nothing to eat in the house. Janson helped his mother, but he was really staying around in case his father came back and caused trouble.

Sil said she was going out to play in the fields, but the moment she was out of sight, she ran into town as fast as her little feet would carry her. She wanted to find her daddy, to bring him home. She knew where she'd find him . . . at Tippy's Saloon.

"Daddy, please come home," Sil Leidenburg begged.

An old farmer called from across the room, "Leidenburg, get your kid out of here!"

Thomas Leidenburg looked down at his daughter. "I'll be right home. Jez tell your ma that I'm not hungry."

"Please come home, Daddy. Please, Momma needs you," Sil begged.

"Go on now, scoot. Jez goin' to have me one more drink, then I'll be home."

"Stop drinking, Daddy. Stop drinking," she begged, holding onto his leg.

He looked down, feeling guilt at his daughter finding him in the saloon and embarrassment at the situation in front of his drinking buddies. "Go on home, Sil. I'll be there soon."

He pushed Sil out through the saloon doors without seeing the tears in her eyes.

Just then, Eulla Mae Springer came by, carrying a bag of groceries. "What's wrong, child?" she asked Sil. "Something bad happen?"

A loud crash followed by drunken laughter came from inside the saloon. Eulla Mae looked through the window and saw that Sil's father had fallen over a table, spilling everyone's drinks.

"Come on, child. I'll walk you home."

Sil poured out her heart on the way, and at the edge of the Leidenburg driveway, Eulla Mae offered the bag of groceries to the little girl.

"Give these to your momma, girl. You need to be

eatin' right. How you goin' to learn in school if you're hungry?"

"Don't go to school. Pa won't let us."

Eulla Mae felt like crying herself, but she had to be strong for the child's sake. She reached into her purse and took out a five-dollar bill.

"Give this money to your momma."

Sil's eyes widened at the sight of the bill. "But that's five dollars, Mrs. Springer!"

"Just don't give it to your Pa. If he asks you if you have any money, just lie to him and say no."

Sil looked at her. "It ain't right to lie, Mrs. Springer."

Eulla Mae picked the girl up and hugged her. "Good Lord will forgive you for lying. Your pa ain't thinkin' right."

Janson came out, and Eulla Mae sat down with both of them to explain that their daddy was sick and needed help.

"He's so mean to us when he's drinkin'," said Janson.

"I know it, honey child. That's the sickness inside of him."

"Will he ever change?" Sil asked.

"I know it's hard to live with him right now, but you got to show him you still love him and want him to get better. He'll change."

Tears began to well up in Janson's eyes. "Life with him isn't fun anymore."

Eulla Mae took him gently by the shoulders. "The

strange thing is that fun on this earth is like that old magician's trick. It's just an illusion."

Eulla Mae held back her own tears. She hugged both children tightly. After a few moments the children relaxed a little in her arms. She smiled into their worried faces and squeezed their hands.

"Now, take this bag of groceries in to your momma. Go on." Eulla Mae struggled to her feet. Her joints had a touch of arthritis.

"But Ma won't accept charity, Mrs. Springer."

Eulla Mae laughed. "Just remind her that she helped Maurice and me that time we both had the fever. I'm just returning the favor."

Eulla Mae walked off down the road, humming. Sil watched her go until she was out of sight in the fading light. A single tear made its way down Janson's face. He put his arm around his sister and hugged her tight.

From the dark, through the trees and on the wind, they heard Eulla Mae's voice singing the old gospel song "Nobody Knows the Trouble I've Seen." It seemed to light the path back toward their house, showing that all was not lost, that the best in life was yet to be found.

The soulful sound of Eulla Mae's voice wrapped a blanket of strength and security around them as they headed toward their troubled home.

CHAPTER 22

EVENING AT THE YOUNGUNS'

Across the ridge from the Leidenburg farm, Terry was sitting in the outhouse, trying to read the Sears catalog by lamplight. Actually, it was pretty hard to do since the pages had been cut up into quarters to use as toilet paper, but Terry was just killing time before going up to bed.

They'd made a mess of the kitchen, cooking dinner. Mrs. Campbell had brought around a big baking chicken, and Pa had told Terry to clean the feathers off it.

So Terry had gotten out Pa's razor and shaving cream, and after lathering up the bird, he'd shaved it clean. He was proud of himself and got carried away, thinking he was a regular little barber. So when his pa came in and found Terry putting powder and smelling water on the bird—like he'd seen Billy Pickle do at his barbershop—the reverend was fit to be tied.

Terry had apologized, but Pa was so mad that grace consisted of his father saying, "Lord, give me the strength to hold back from wuppin' this auburn-haired wild handful."

That was then and this was now. Terry shrugged his shoulders and continued reading the Sears Catalog.

MOVING PICTURES
WE FURNISH COMPLETE OUTFITS FOR 5-CENT THEATERS

THE MOVING PICTURE BUSINESS has grown to immense proportions, developing into a worldwide enterprise, involving an invested capital of millions of dollars.

Like the advent of the telephone or the graphaphone, the moving picture machine was at first regarded as more or less of a curiosity, but when the possibilities of this new field became better known, it grew more and more into favor with the public and recently has sprung into such popular favor that there is scarcely a city of any size in this country which does not contain . . .

Contain what? Terry wanted to read the rest of the article and flipped through the quarter pages on the outhouse bench. Thinking that he'd found it, he continued reading:

The celebrated H & H Bust Forms are now so perfect that they cannot be detected from the natural bust, whether by sight or touch. Strikingly stylish, a source of relief, delight, and pride to the wearer

Wearer of what? "Bust Forms" didn't make much sense to Terry. He put the stack of quarter pages on his lap, but a bunch of them fell down into the dark hole of no return.

"Dangit," he said, "I hope the rest of the moving picture business didn't fall down there."

He heard a growling at the door. Dangit the dog was trying to butt his head in.

"Sorry, Dangit. Didn't mean to use your name wrong."

He found a more-or-less whole page and read:

WALLPAPER DIRECT TO YOU FROM OUR OWN MILL.
3 CENTS
A DOUBLE ROLL OF 16 YARDS.

That wasn't about moving pictures.

OUR SPECIAL SELF-PRONOUNCING COMBINATION TEACHERS' BIBLE $1.43

Terry gave up hope of ever finding the rest of the moving picture story, which was too bad, since it sounded like a job he could do. Making movies sounded better than going to school and cleaning the dishes. He imagined himself making a movie called "All the Candy in the World" and profiting enough to make the title come true!

As he flipped through the pages, he saw something that affected the safety of his life and limb. It was just what Larry needed to protect his little brother:

BOXING GLOVES

We are the largest handlers of boxing gloves in the United States, selling more gloves direct to the consumer than any other house. We have made the requirements of the pugilist a careful study and you will find that our gloves fit better, last longer, and quality and construction considered, are cheaper than any other gloves on the market.

We send free a copy of the Marquis of Queensbury Rules with every set.

Professional Fighting Gloves $2.22

Striking or punching bags 97 cents

Terry had saved up $3.50 from his paper route this past summer. Sending away for the boxing gloves and punching bag was the least he could do for his brother.

Inside, Larry was getting into his nightshirt. Sherry was already fast asleep, with her blanket in one arm, her Carry Nation dolly in the other, and her thumb stuck deep in her mouth.

She momentarily awoke and said, "Good night, Carry Nation, wherever you are." Larry looked in on her and smiled. She was probably the only girl kid in the whole

U.S. of A. that had named her dolly after the axe-wielding prohibitionist!

Terry tried to tiptoe as quietly as he could past the parlor where Pa was reading the newspaper, but Pa had the ears of a bat! From behind the wall came "the voice." "Do you know what time it is, son?"

"Yes, Pa."

"Shouldn't you be in bed by now?"

"Yes, Pa," Terry said, rolling his eyes.

"Terry, I'm still mad at you for using my razor and shaving cream on the bird."

"Yes, Pa." Now Terry was having fun going through the motions. He was imitating his father and making a face with his answer. He opened his eyes when he heard the rustle of a newspaper.

"So you think this is just a joke, eh?"

Terry put his brain into kid-speed.

"Joke? No, Pa. I was just . . ." Terry was thinking as fast as he could, but nothing would come.

"Speak up! Answer me."

"I heard that the church is going to let the kids put on a Christmas play, and I was just practicing to get a part."

Rev. Youngun looked at his lovable scampster. Yes, there had been an announcement of a church play—he had made it himself during last Sunday's after-sermon announcements. But he knew his son too well.

"Are you telling me the truth, son?"

To fib or not to fib, that was Terry's dilemma.

"Are you telling me the truth, son?" his father asked again, rolling up the newspaper.

"Pa, have you ever done a thing which became another thing which made the first untrue thing a true thing?"

Rev. Youngun closed his eyes for a moment. "Go on."

"Well, maybe somewheres in the back of my brain I was thinkin' about your sermonizing about the baby Jesus play and it made me do things that I normally wouldn't have done if I hadn't been thinkin' about what you asked me to think about when you . . ."

Rev. Youngun knew where this was leading. Terry could talk circles around him every time. The only thing he could think to say was the all-purpose parents' escape. "I want you to say your prayers right now and go to sleep."

"Yes, Pa," Terry said. His pa had forgotten what had started the whole conversation.

Since Pa slept in the first-floor bedroom, he didn't venture upstairs all that much. It was the Youngun kids' responsibility to keep things clean, but it was really a case of out of sight, out of mind. It always looked a mess up there.

Larry tried to keep things neat, and Sherry did her little best, but Terry would drop everything anywhere as it came off: shirt on the steps, pants on the floor, underwear hung on the doorknobs, and socks kicked off anywhere.

Pa had said to pray, but Terry wasn't all that concerned about it. He wasn't like Sherry, who'd pray at the drop of a hat. Why, she'd pray for rain, sleet, sun, and good and bad weather. It didn't seem to matter to her; she just liked to pray.

His older brother, Larry, said the prayers he'd been taught by Ma and read the Bible before bed, like Pa asked him to. "You're a good boy," Pa always told Larry after he finished his two-minute prayer—which was about two minutes too long, in Terry's book.

His older brother was a good guy, and if he needed to read the Bible and pray each night to give him the strength to protect his little brother from Red Shaughnessy, then that was fine with Terry. Just in case the prayin' wasn't strong enough, however, Terry was going to get him boxing gloves and a punching bag. He took a quick peek at the Sears' ads and smiled.

Saying the same prayer every night was not something that Terry liked to do. As a matter of fact, he got so tired of it that he had Larry write his evening prayer out for him.

Terry had hidden the prayer sheet under his pillow. As he had done for the past several months, he pulled it out and knelt down in front of the bed.

He looked at the piece of paper and said, "Dear Lord, them's my sentiments exactly."

Then he jumped under the covers and put his hands behind his head in the dark, thinking about the movie he wanted to make, "All the Candy in the World." *Now that was something to pray for and dream about,* he said to himself as he drifted off.

CHAPTER 23

THE THREAT

The phone rang in the kitchen while Laura was writing at her desk. After three more rings, she looked up. "Will you answer it, Manly?"

Getting no reply, she put her pencil down and walked quickly to the kitchen. "Hello," she said, but there was no reply. "Hello, who is this, please?"

A deep, gruff, man's voice said, "Quit causin' trouble."

"I beg your pardon?"

"You heard me. Quit writin' trash and defendin' trash."

"Who is this?" Laura demanded.

"You know."

"No, I don't know, and I'm going to hang up."

"We're watchin' you," the man whispered. "We're watchin' you right now."

Laura shivered and looked out the window. "If this is a joke, I don't like it."

"The Klan doesn't joke, lady," the man whispered. "If

you don't stop sidin' with the wrong side, we're gonna come pay you a visit."

"Good-bye," Laura said, hanging the phone up.

Disgusted with the caller, she stood in the kitchen, looking out the window. Then the phone rang again.

"Hello," she said in a curt voice.

"I wasn't finished," the voice whispered. "We won't let you ruin the harvests. You need to leave the farm kids alone."

"Why don't you leave me alone?"

"Go look on your front door. We left a message for you." Then the phone clicked off, and Laura was left holding the receiver in her hand.

Laura hung the phone up and debated whether she should go to the front door or not. *Where is Manly?* she asked herself.

"Manly!" she shouted out.

"I'm out in the barn," came a faint reply.

Laura opened the back porch door and saw Manly standing with a lantern in his hand. "You need somethin', Laura?"

"I just had a strange call and it scared me."

Manly closed the barn door. "Who was it?" he asked, walking toward the house.

"Said he was with the Klan, and said to go look on the front door."

Manly took her back inside the kitchen and closed the door. He turned off the lantern and reached behind the pantry door. "What are you looking for?" Laura asked.

"My shotgun," he said, bringing it out. Without saying another word, he went to the front door and opened it. Laura stood in the doorway of the kitchen.

"See anything?" she asked.

Manly pulled the note off the door and handed it to Laura. "Seems like someone don't like you," he said.

Laura looked at the crudely written note which said:

LEAVE OUR KIDS A LONE AND LEVE MISSOURA YOU TRATER!

Laura crumpled the paper up. "This is what I'm fighting," she said. "Ignorance and prejudice . . . they go hand in hand in this life."

"You want me to call the sheriff and report this?" Manly asked.

"No, anybody who'd call and threaten is just all talk. They're trying to scare me into silence, and it won't work."

"I could have told them that," Manly chuckled.

"I'm serious, Manly. That call has inspired me."

"Inspired you? What on earth are you talkin' 'bout, woman?"

"Every time I get depressed or think the odds are against me, I'm going to think about that gutless voice on the phone."

She walked into the darkened parlor and stood by the fireplace. Setting the crumpled message on the stone hearth, she struck a match and burned it. As the flame danced in the darkened room, she nodded and said to Manly, "This message of ignorance is my mission."

Across the hills, the Grand Dragon smiled as he thought about the phone call. *That ought to shut her up,* he thought. *And if it don't, then maybe we'll have to do a little night ridin' and burnin' at her Apple Hill Farm.*

CHAPTER 24

CAN YOU READ, BOY?

Laura Ingalls Wilder was on a mission. She traveled the dirt roads in search of what she had begun calling the Children of Promise, telling them to go to school. There were yelling matches and threats from parents, but she stood her ground.

One of the reasons she went at it with such intensity was that Rose had gone back to school in New Orleans. She wouldn't see her daughter again until Thanksgiving and already missed her.

Manly had come up with the idea of putting up groups of five signs, spaced out on the road, four signs in sequence to get your attention and the fifth with the message. Having written several rhymes, Laura's favorite was:

Reading and writing,	(Sign One)
And arithmetic too,	(Sign Two)
Your friends go to school,	(Sign Three)

So why don't you?   (Sign Four)
GO TO SCHOOL!   (Sign Five)

Laura and some of her friends walked, rode horseback, drove her buggy, and rode in her 1905 Oldsmobile through the hollows and between the ridges.

Automobiles were noisy machines that were uncertain at best. If you had a car that could climb a hill without stalling, you were the envy of all the neighbors. Most of them had to "tack" uphill, like sailing a boat into the wind.

Laura loved her new Oldsmobile, with its ten horsepower single-cylinder engine under the seat. She was fascinated with cars, and when she saw the 1905 Olds with the French-type hood concealing the water and gas tanks, she had to have one. It was heavier, ran faster, and seemed better suited for the Ozark roads than other models.

At that time, there were a lot of strange cars with stranger names belching smoke and careening down the bumpy roads. There was the Ajax, the Black Crow, the Centaur, the De Tamble, and the Pungs-Finch, the Wheel-Within-Wheel. There were cars named after cards, such as the Ace, King, Queen, and Jaxon, and some with animal names, such as the Deere, Colt, Dragon, Wolf, Lion, and Wolverine.

Just being able to go to town and back was an accomplishment, so in the spirit of American advertising there were cars named Glide, Long Distance, Success, Marvel, Great, and the Only. But like a lot of advertising, not all of it was truthful, except maybe for the car called the Dodo.

When the tires wore down, people just pumped a mastic filler into them which rendered them puncture proof! The only problem was that standing on a hot day filled with the glutinous mass and not inflated, the tires had a tendency to flatten and remain like that for several miles.

If a mastic-filled tire burst, the jelly just spurted into the air and congealed into thin shreds. It looked as if a feather mattress had exploded on the road!

As Laura came up over the crest of the hill, she was so deep in thought that she didn't notice the chicken crossing the road until it was too late and a bunch of feathers filled the air. All she heard was one loud, last squawk from the chicken.

Laura looked down at the sea of feathers around her and couldn't help thinking about all those chicken-crossing-the-road jokes.

"The joke's on you," she laughed.

"What the heck you laughing about? You done runned over my best chicken!"

With a look of concern on her face, she shook her head. "I'm sorry, Mr. Swenson. I'll be glad to pay you for your . . ."

He cut her off. "You danged tin-can motor-car tourists! That was my prize hen! You shore did it now, you did!"

He picked up the dead chicken. Laura had to suppress a smile, thinking to herself, *Why did the chicken cross the road? To be run over by Laura Wilder!*

"I said I'm sorry, but it was an accident. What do you consider your prize hen worth?"

Swenson shook his head and walked in a circle, talking to himself. "This here's a prize bird. Her pedigree goes back to Plymouth Rock. Why, I don't think George Washington himself could replace her."

It was all part of a bargaining session. Stretch the truth, add some hype, puff and strut and fib a little, till you got the price you wanted.

Laura had been through the game many times before and just wanted to cut to the chase. "How much do I owe you?"

He ignored her question and went right on moaning and complaining. "And the worst of all, this here hen's name is Matilda. She was the family pet, just like a regular member of the family."

"How much do you want for the damages? I'm sure you've got a price in mind."

"You know how much Matilda is, er—was worth? Why let me just tell ya. . . ."

Mr. Swenson then embarked on an Ozark eulogy over Matilda, the hen who, by the end of the sermon, could all but talk, heal the sick and lame, and walk on water to get to her nest.

Laura began wondering if she had enough money in her purse.

"Mr. Swenson, I've got to be going. Could you just

tell me what's the best price you can do for . . . for Matilda?"

"Matilda's goin' to cost you an arm and a leg, lady."

"If you throw in the drumsticks and breasts, what is your price?"

Swenson had her where he wanted her. "I won't take a penny less than fifty cents!"

Laura pulled out the money and handed it to him, then took Matilda and tossed her on the floorboard. Nothing wrong with the chicken!

Swenson took out his glasses to look at and bite the coins and make sure he wasn't getting Yankeed. Finding they were real, he then took a clear look at Laura.

A boy came running up to the car and walked around it. It was obvious that the car thrilled him, but he would barely touch it.

"Ma'am, how much power does your car have?" the boy asked.

"This Oldsmobile has ten horsepower in the engine," she said.

"You mean to tell me they be ten horses' power in that motorized buggy? 'Tain't safe. Supposin' that thing gits out of control? You got a whip to control it?"

Laura laughed. "Cars don't eat oats, son. They eat gas . . . and lots of it. But a whip? No, you just take your foot off the gas and it'll slow down."

The boy then noticed that his pa was looking at Laura and getting all red faced. "What's wrong, Pa?" the boy asked.

"Nothin'. Be quiet." He looked at Laura. "You're the

woman all the farmers be talkin' about. Leave my boy alone and get off my property!"

Laura looked at him. "Mr. Swenson, the road doesn't belong to you, so I can sit here as long as I please. Why isn't your boy in school?"

The boy started to speak, but his father hushed him with a stern look.

"Junior don't need to know how to read," said the old farmer. "He's going to be a farmer like me."

"Here," she said, handing him a copy of the Missouri law on children attending school. "You're breaking the law. Your son should be in school. Read this."

Swenson spit on the ground. "It's radicals like you which is tryin' to hurt this country. Why don't you go on back to where you came from?"

"I intend to go home right after this," Laura shot back.

Swenson looked at her with venom in his eyes. "I mean back to whatever foreign country sent you to disrupt us." He looked at her hair. It had just a hint of red from the afternoon sun. "You be a bit of a redhead. Might you be a Catholic?"

"Oh, hardly," she laughed. "Even if I was, what would that have to do with your boy going to school?"

Swenson kicked the dirt. "I heard 'bout that teacher at school."

"You've been listening too much to the Klan and not enough to common sense." She looked at Junior, who was watching it all.

Junior was caught between his father and his future, whether he knew it or not. Laura thought he knew it.

Laura said to him, "Son, have you ever been to school?"

Before his father could stop him, he answered, "Couple days here and there when Paps and Ma gots to go to town on farm business. I go there and just sit."

"Can you read, boy?" she asked tenderly.

"No, ma'am. I can't."

Laura turned to his father. "Did you read what the law says? Your son has to attend school."

The farmer crumpled the flyer and tossed it under Laura's car. "I ain't goin' to pay that no mind. Might be about anything."

"Anything? Did you read it?"

The old farmer spit again. "Can't read, but I get by. That's the way I was raised."

"Why don't you want to read? You can still learn!"

"Can't teach an old dog new tricks, so I best be leavin' well 'nough alone. Now you be gettin' off my land."

"I'm on the public road. Son, you want me to take you to school today, like the law says?"

Swenson took his son by the collar and walked into the fields, away from Laura.

"You can't hide from it forever," she shouted after Swenson. "One day your son's going to blame you for making him into an ignorant!"

Swenson stopped, turned, and glared at her. "We at least got our pride and know when to leave others alone. It'll be you to blame if the farmers don't get their harvest in on time!"

Laura didn't say anything more. She watched them walk off, the ignorant leading a child of promise into another generation of ignorance, offering him no choice.

CHAPTER 25

THE FEED STORE

While Laura was busy running over Swenson's chicken, Manly went to the feed store in Mansfield and ran into a wall of silence. Even the owner, Thomas Campbell, treated him like an outcast.

"Morning, Thomas. Any news today?"

That was the same greeting that Manly had used for years. Normally, Thomas Campbell would bring him up-to-date on farm news and gossip, but today was different.

"What you need, Manly?" Campbell asked, suddenly finding everything to do but look Manly in the eye.

There were several local farmers sitting near the back wall. They went silent when they saw Manly.

"I said, 'Morning, Thomas. Any news today?' Didn't you hear me?"

"I heard you, Manly, but I don't have to answer you. Just do your business and go about your way. Your wife is threatening to hurt the harvest."

On the wall behind the counter was a picture of

Laura stuck on a dart board. One of her articles was pinned next to it, crossed out in red.

Manly grabbed the sack of feed he'd come for. "Keeping kids in school is going to hurt the harvest? I don't think so."

Edwin Ebenezer, a local veteran and general stick-his-nose-into-anything, shouted from the back of the store. "Who can afford to hire helpers if they don't bring in the harvest? Most everyone 'round here is already on credit to Campbell here, so no one's got extra money to waste on hired hands."

Manly paid for the feed and turned to Ebenezer. "Then they're poor farmers if they don't plan ahead."

Campbell slammed the cash register shut. "Not everyone's got money like the Wilders, or a farm like Apple Hill."

"No, that's right," Manly said cautiously. " 'Cause not everyone is willing to sacrifice and put off new clothes or go a bit hungry to get ahead." He looked Campbell in the eye. "I paid all my bills to you, even when it kept us hungry."

A local tenant farmer named Billy Lee Jones stood up in the back. "I hear your wife pushes you around, Manly Wilder," he said in an obnoxious, needling voice.

Manly laughed. He'd been down this road before. "Billy Lee, if you'd push yourself away from the icebox more often, you'd have more room to talk."

Ebenezer came to the front. "You ain't never had a problem in your life."

Manly dropped the feed sack on the floor and spun

around on Ebenezer. "You're just talkin' horse manure. My wife and I came here with nothin', and we built somethin'. We'd lost everything in the Dakotas—our crops, our house, and a baby son. But I learned from my mistakes. I can't help it if you're jealous, but I won't let you be spreadin' untruths."

The bell above the front door tinkled and Father Walsh walked in. "Afternoon, lads," he said in his distinctive Irish brogue.

"Hi, Father Walsh," Manly said. "You lookin' for something to feed your flock?"

Father Walsh smiled. "You got a good sense of humor, Manly. Sure you don't have a touch of the Irish in ya?" he laughed.

Billy Lee shouted from the back, "He's a Catholic lover so he's probably got some Irish in him." Ebenezer laughed along with Billy Lee.

Father Walsh's mood changed. "I feel sorry for you, Billy Lee. I'll pray for you."

He handed his order to Campbell. "I'll be back to pick it up in about an hour. Good to see you, Manly."

Manly picked up his feed sack and left the store, "Thanks for selling me the feed, Campbell. You ought to learn some manners, like Evans at the hardware store."

"You be buying your goods there now?" Campbell asked with a weary eye.

"You don't sell lumber," Manly snapped back.

"What you building?" Ebenezer jeered. "A wall around your farm for protection?"

"No," Manly said. "Just putting on a simple roof." As he left, he bumped into Thomas Leidenburg, who had come to buy more supplies on credit.

Campbell listened to the story of why Leidenburg needed credit, but knew that Leidenburg had drunk up the farm money.

Campbell knew he had humiliated Manly, who had always paid his bills, never fibbed when times were tough, and paid interest on those few times he needed to be carried for a month or so. It wasn't right, and he knew he would have to apologize to Manly later. You can't treat good customers that way, or they'll take their business elsewhere. Even if he did disagree with his wife's writings.

"Just give me the feed until my harvest comes in. You know I'm good for it, Campbell," begged Leidenburg.

Reaching for his accounts ledger, Campbell looked up Leidenburg's record. "Let's see here. Says you already owe over five hundred and forty-three dollars for the past eighteen months."

Leidenburg stepped back. "But I've been payin' you interest!"

Campbell just shook his head. "How you ever goin' to get the balance paid off? It would take all the money from your apple crop and then some to pay it!"

Leidenburg panicked. "I've been workin' hard, usin' all my strength to pay you back. I don't do nothing else but work."

"And drink and beat your wife," Ebenezer added. "If

you'd turn your apples into hard cider, then you could make money and stay drunk all year long!"

Out front, a woman posted a handbill on the front window of the feed store. Campbell walked out. "What are you putting up there, Mrs. Peterson?"

The sheriff's wife handed him a copy from the stack in her hand. "It's time the children were kept in school. There's a law, you know."

"Indeed there is," Campbell chuckled. "But is your husband goin' to be the first sheriff in county history to arrest farmers for havin' their children work on the farm?"

"He and I have been arguing about that, but the law's the law." She strutted away to the next store, to post another handbill.

Campbell took it into the store and read it. With only two weeks to go before the harvest, there was no time to bring in other men from Springfield to work the crops. With the baling and picking machines already contracted for and the approaching bad weather, any delay could destroy the economy of the town.

"What's it say?" Billy Lee asked from the back of the room.

"It's a copy of the Missouri State law on children attending school and a message from Laura Wilder." He handed it to Billy Lee, "Here, read it for yourself."

Billy Lee handed it back. "You read it to me. I can't read worth a lick," he laughed, thinking he was funny.

Campbell put on his reading glasses. "It says, 'Every

child has promise. No child should be denied an education. If you can't read or write, is that the way you want your children to grow up? Do you want them to be too dumb to even read the state law? And if someone else is reading this to you, don't you feel helpless to events that you can't even read about?"

Campbell lowered the handbill and looked at the assembled men. He rubbed his eyes, then continued. "Do not keep your children out of school. Not only is it against the law, it is cruel and mean to deny your children the opportunity to advance themselves. Harvest their minds. Don't have them work the harvest when they should be in school."

Billy Lee spoke up first. "That woman's trouble."

"She's crazy," Ebenezer said loudly.

"First frost is coming soon. Has everyone got all their crops in yet?" Campbell asked, taking his reading glasses off.

"You know better," said Leidenburg. "If it weren't for that durned Wilder woman, I'd have had my apple crop in by now, but she's got my old lady and kids all riled up!"

"If the farmers of Wright County lose their crops 'cause of her writin', there's goin' to be trouble!" said Billy Lee.

"I heard the Klan's talkin' 'bout night ridin' on Apple Hill if she don't shut her durned mouth," grumbled Campbell.

"Serve her and that whipped husband of hers right.

What's she think kids are on this earth for?" the old farmer said, after spitting into the spittoon. "What good are they if you can't raise 'em to work on the farm?"

"Yeah, and books are a waste of money," Leidenburg said as he left the feed store and headed toward Tippy's to get a drink.

At the saloon door, Eulla Mae confronted him. "You ought to be ashamed of yourself, Thomas Leidenburg. Your children know you're the town drunk. You got the devil inside, leading you wrong."

"No, Eulla Mae," he said, seeing the salvation of the bottles behind the bar only a few feet ahead. "I just like to drink. I'm not hurtin' anyone."

"No," she said, shaking her head, "you're not hurtin' anyone. You're hurtin' everyone around you."

She walked off, leaving him to face only himself. There was no one between him and the bar except what was left of the man that used to be. Leidenburg pushed that vision aside and went into the saloon.

"Give me another drink," Leidenburg said loudly.

O'Shea put his book down and looked at Leidenburg. "You've had too much to drink. Go home and sober up."

Leidenburg started to fuss, and O'Shea threw him out of the saloon. He looked at the drunkard and said, "You won't be drinkin' in here no more. It's killin' you." O'Shea suddenly felt good inside, for the first time in months.

Thomas Huleatt, the owner of the saloon, shouted

out to him from the top of the stairs, "O'Shea, get back behind the bar and pour those customers' drinks."

"I won't be pourin' no more drinks," O'Shea said, taking off his apron. "I'm going back to workin' the timber with me lads in the Hardacres."

CHAPTER 26

THE PLAN

Sitting in the corner of Tippy's Saloon were the three Klan members, hunched over the table, whispering among themselves.

"That Wilder woman is still out hurtin' the harvest," the thin man said, shaking his head.

"Yeah, she didn't scare off none, even after your call," the stocky man nodded. "What are we gonna do, boss?"

Scratching his bushy eyebrows, the Grand Dragon whispered, "We're gonna call a rally . . . just like they do in St. Louis."

"A rally?" the thin man whispered. "But there's only three of us."

"Don't forget the three boys from over in Norwood," the stocky man added.

"Three or six, it don't matter. When folks see us in our robes and hoods, three will look like three hundred. It's fear. They're scared of the dark and what they don't know."

"And no one knows who we are!" the thin man bragged loudly.

"Shut up, you fool!" the Klan leader snapped, leaning closer to the two men. "If folks learn that we're the local Klan, then they wouldn't be scared of us."

"I heard some ol' boys drinkin' behind the livery, sayin' they heard that there were thousands of Klan members in the Ozarks," the stocky man grinned.

"One day there will be," the Klan leader said coldly. "And that's why we're gonna call a rally."

"A recruitin' rally?" the thin man asked.

"Naw, people join after they see a cross burn. They get so excited thinkin' 'bout wearin' a hood and scarin' people that in St. Louis they join up right on the spot."

"How we gonna get the word out?" the thin man asked.

"We're gonna pay a visit tomorrow night to that newspaper editor. I want him to run a story about the rally," the Grand Dragon said.

"I don't think he will," the stocky man said.

"He will."

"Why you so sure?" the stocky man asked.

" 'Cause if he don't, I got a bullet with his name on it sittin' in my pistol," he said, patting his coat pocket.

CHAPTER 27

ROUND TWO

Terry Youngun did a double take in the school play area. Sweet walked by, carrying a little wicker cage. Inside were the "porcupine eggs," the sweet gum balls that he'd sold him!

"Sweet, what are you doing? I told you to take them porcupine eggs home and hide 'em," Terry exclaimed, running after his friend.

Sweet turned. "Oh, hi, Terry. I'm going to show them to the class."

Terry had to think of something fast. "You ever heard of PCF?" he asked, with a worried look on his face.

Sweet shook his head. " 'PCF'? What's that?"

"PCF stands for Porcupine Class Fever. Those eggs will never hatch if you put them in front of a class of humans. Says so right in the Sears catalog."

Now, most folks took anything that was in the Sears catalog as gospel, so Sweet had to think about it. "What should I do with 'em, then?"

Relief swept across Terry's face. "Just hide 'em under

the building until school's over. Then take 'em home and put 'em in the closet."

Terry skipped away, having just saved himself from another jam. *That was close,* he thought.

Li called him over. "Terry, you got any of Davy Crockett's hair with you? I got two pennies," he said, holding up the shiny coins.

The two pennies stared back at him, and Terry couldn't resist. "I got some hidden behind the school. How much you want?"

Li counted the coins in his hand, just to make sure. "Two cents' worth. How much will that get me?"

Terry acted offended. "You ought to be giving me a quarter for a single hair, but since you're my friend, I'll treat you right. Be right back," he said, skipping off behind the building.

Once out of sight, Terry pulled out his trusty pocketknife and began cutting off a lock of his hair. He wrapped it in a leaf and, just in case Sweet had some more money to spend, he cut an extra lock and put it in his pocket.

Li was waiting near the marbles circle, watching some of the boys shoot for cat's-eyes. Terry came around the corner as if he were going to the bank.

"You got it?" he asked Terry.

"Yeah, but I hate to sell it so cheap," he said, pulling out the leaf-wrapped lock of hair.

Li looked at the auburn hair closely, then up at Terry's auburn mop of hair. There was an obvious chop mark on Terry's bangs. Terry looked up with one eye closed and quickly combed his fingers through his hair to hide the cut.

"This hair's the same color as yours!" Li said. "You sure this is Davy Crockett's hair?"

Terry looked offended. "Are you makin' fun of the great Davy Crockett, the greatest auburn-haired Indian fighter that ever lived?"

Li stammered, "No, I . . . I . . ."

Terry puffed out his chest with indignation. "Just give me back that hair. I was going to send it to the museum in St. Louis, but you said you wanted to buy it. You're makin' fun of a great man."

"Sorry, Terry, it just looked like your hair," Li said. "Here's my two cents."

"Looks can be deceiving," Terry said, pocketing the money.

"What's it going to be worth?" Li whispered.

Terry put his hand on Li's shoulder. "Can't even place a value on something so rare," he said, skipping away.

Miss O'Conner came out onto the steps and rang the bell. The children tumbled in and took their seats.

"It's now time for our spelling bee. I'll begin with the older children," Miss O'Conner said. "I've written down a list of words that I'm going to ask you to spell."

The children groaned, and Little James and Terry slid down in their seats. Larry and Frenchie gulped and looked around. Only the Hardacres boys looked confident.

"All right, here's the first word for . . . Frenchie. You spell the word *recipe*."

Frenchie closed his eyes. "R . . . es . . . c . . . e . . . e . . . p . . . ee."

Miss O'Conner shook her head. "Wrong. You should read your McGuffey and practice your spelling. Let's see, who's next?" She looked at Missouri. "Missouri, you try."

Missouri shook her head. "Don't know how to spell it and don't know what the word means."

Miss O'Conner looked at Sweet. "How about you?"

Sweet chewed the inside of his mouth. "Rec . . . sip . . . pee."

"Wrong," the teacher said. "Larry Youngun, can you spell it?"

Larry closed his eyes and concentrated. "Re . . . c . . . i . . . p . . . ee." He thought he had gotten it wrong.

"Almost," Miss O'Conner said, shaking her head. She looked at Red Shaughnessy, "Red, want to give it a try?"

Red stood up. "Certainly, Miss O'Conner. The word is *recipe* and it's spelled, rec . . . ipe."

Miss O'Conner smiled brightly. "That's right! Very good, Red. I'm proud of you."

This continued on, word after word. Larry got a few right, Missouri didn't try, and Frenchie got so frustrated that he began mixing French and English.

The strange thing was that Red, Wiley, and Gene— the boys from the Hardacres—got every word right!

They had always been the worst students, but now they were making everyone else look like dunces!

Miss O'Conner was so proud that she slipped in and out of her Irish brogue in her congratulations, until by the end of class it was hard to understand her. To make matters worse, she gave each of the three Hardacres boys a piece of candy and let them go to afternoon recess early.

When the rest of the class was allowed to leave, Red, Wiley, and Gene were standing by the steps.

"Here come the dumbos," Red laughed, looking at Larry, Terry, and Little James. "Dumb, dumb, and dumber."

"Ignore them," Larry said quietly, trying to move his brother and Little James in the other direction.

"Just 'cause your mother dropped you on your head, doesn't mean we have to be nice to you," jeered Terry.

Larry closed his eyes, hoping Red hadn't heard it. No such luck.

"What did you say, shrimp?" Red screamed, stepping boldly over, pushing students out of the way.

Terry threw a bunch of air punches. "Let me at 'em. Let me at 'em."

Larry blocked Red and held his brother back. "Leave him alone, Red. You started it."

Red put his face up to Larry's. "I told you to stay out of my way, preacher's boy. You already got one black eye."

"Fightin's not right," Larry said. "You leave us alone."

"Hey, Wiley," Red said. "I told you preacher's boy is chicken!" Without warning, he swung his fist toward Larry's stomach.

Larry blocked it and held onto Red's arm. "I said I didn't want to fight." He let go of his arm, but Red swung again the moment it was released.

Larry ducked and grabbed Red's arm, twisting it around behind his back.

"Let go! No fair!" Red screamed.

"I said I didn't want to fight. Leave us alone."

Terry and Little James stood behind Larry, wishing they were invisible. *Where is my Sears package*? Terry wondered.

As Larry turned to leave, Wiley walked over and stuck his foot out and Red pushed him over. "Come on, preacher's boy," Red laughed. "I'm going to be here every day until you fight."

Larry got up and dusted himself off. "My pa says, 'Blessed are the meek: for they shall inherit the earth.' "

Red pushed up against him. "And my pa says 'hit first and hard.' "

"I feel sorry for you, Red," Larry said, turning away. Red let go with a roundhouse punch onto Larry's other eye, knocking him down.

"Get up and fight, you chicken," Red sneered, standing over him.

"Kick him, Red! Kick him!" urged Gene Buchanan.

Miss O'Conner came to the back door, "Boys, boys,

that's enough!" She came down and stood between them. "What's this all about?"

This time Larry didn't hold back. "I told him that I didn't want to fight and to leave my little brother and Little James alone."

"His little brother called me a name!" Red exclaimed.

"He started it!" Terry piped up.

Miss O'Conner looked at Red and then at Larry. "You two boys will not be allowed to take recess until you settle your differences. I don't care if it takes all year. There will be no more fighting."

The rest of the afternoon went very slowly. Larry's eye had swollen shut, and after school he didn't want to walk home with the rest of the gang.

At Willow Creek Bridge, he sat on the rail, looking at the water, lost in thought. He'd turned his cheek once and gotten a black eye. Now he'd turned it again and his other eye was swollen shut. He had no more cheeks to turn! What should he do?

"What are you thinking about, son?" his father asked from behind him.

Larry was embarrassed to turn around and show his black eye. "Oh, Pa, I'm just thinkin' 'bout nothin'."

Rev. Youngun turned his son around and saw the swollen eye. "Another fight?" he asked quietly.

Larry started to break down and hugged his father. "Pa, I did what you said, but it hurts. It don't make sense not to defend yourself."

Rev. Youngun put his arm around his son and walked

him down the dusty road toward their home. "I've been in your shoes, Larry. I really have."

Larry looked up through his one good eye. "Did you ever have to face a fight, Pa?"

Rev. Youngun smiled. "I took this same walk with my father when I was little, because a boy was picking on me at school."

"What'd you do?" Larry asked, kicking a dirt clod to the side of the road.

"My father said that the Bible doesn't say a thing about not defending yourself. If you've honestly done all you can not to fight, then you've done all you can in the Lord's eyes."

"For real, Pa?"

"For real. I don't want you picking fights, using curse words, or being rude to ladies. But that doesn't mean you have to be abused or allow your family to suffer abuse."

"What should I do, Pa? Red says he's goin' to wait for me every day."

"I can't tell you what to do, but I will tell you that the Bible says that 'The Lord lifteth up the meek: he casteth the wicked down to the ground.' If Red Shaughnessy will not leave you alone and tries to fight you again, then it may be necessary to put him on the ground."

"Should I hit him, Pa?"

"I didn't say that. Just use your best judgment at the time. You'll know what's right."

CHAPTER 28

CLICK, CLICK, CLICK

I told you we're watching you," came the voice from under the Klan hood at the back door of the *Mansfield Monitor*. Two other hooded intruders of the night were behind him.

"I don't have time for your childish games," Summers huffed, starting to push the door closed in the man's face.

"Maybe you have time for this," he growled, pulling a Colt out from under the robe.

Summers stared at the end of the barrel. "No need for that," he said, with a false air of bravery.

"Here's what you need!" the stranger said, cocking the hammer.

A bead of sweat appeared above Summers's left eye, followed by another and another. The seconds ticked by as slowly as hours.

"Don't shoot me," he finally whispered.

"Say please," laughed the tall one standing in the back.

"Pl . . . pl . . . please," Summers whimpered. He closed his eyes and thought a prayer as the trigger was pulled.

Click!

Click, click, click!

Click, click!

The three hooded men laughed. The gun was empty. Summers opened his eyes and pushed forward.

The hooded leader punched him in the stomach. "Don't get too brave too fast, Mr. News-pa-per-man," he said. He tossed a bullet at Summers's feet.

"This one's got your name on it," he laughed, hitting Summers again. "Just remember, we're watching you!"

A flyer was shoved into his hands by the short, hooded man. "We're callin' a rally, and we want you to put it on the first page of your paper."

The three intruders vanished as quickly as they'd arrived. Summers read and reread the crudely written flyer about the Klan rally called for Friday night to "protect the harvest and American education."

The *click, click, click* echoed in Summers's mind. What should he do? This was something he couldn't ignore, something he'd never had to confront before.

CHAPTER 29

BRING YOUR BELLS!

By the next afternoon, the Klan rally to be held in the field outside of town was common knowledge. Most folks were treating it as a lark.

For many of them, it was just something to do.

Laura would have none of it. She got on the phone, called every woman she knew, and invited them all to the farm. The phone operator took it upon herself to call others and spread the word.

The word went out to "bring your bells." School bell, cowbell or dinner bell, it didn't matter. Just bring your bells!

As she waited for the women to arrive, Laura wondered if her anger and ego had unleashed this problem. *Would the Klan even be listened to if I hadn't tried to force my views*? she asked herself. Would it really change anything in the course of life if she forced all the children to go to school?

When the women arrived at Apple Hill in buggies, wagons, and a variety of automobiles, Laura no longer felt alone. She walked out onto the front porch and looked at her friends.

"Did you bring your bells, girls?" she shouted.

The ringing of the bells was almost deafening!

A breeze picked up the leaves on the porch as winter sent a warning of its coming. The first frost had already touched the top of the ridges. A freeze was sure to follow.

"Hope you got your apple crop in, Laura," said Mrs. Bedal as she came up the stairs. "There's a good freeze in the air, and it'll ruin whatever you ain't got in yet!"

"Most of ours is in. Don't you worry," Laura said, patting her on the back.

After all the women had entered, Laura went back on the porch to see if there were any stragglers. Manly pulled his wagon to a stop at the front steps.

"Laura, I'm going to go into town while you ladies have your meeting."

She laughed. "Pick me up a copy of today's paper, will you?"

Manly said he would and rode down the drive. Laura was just about to go back inside when she saw another woman walking up the creek path. As the woman got closer she stopped, as if hesitating.

Laura recognized Silvia Leidenburg and went out to greet her. "I'm glad you came, Silvia. I'm so glad you came," she said, walking her up the stairs.

Silvia had let her hair dangle over her black eye to hide her embarrassment. "I want my children to go to school, Laura. I want them to go to school."

Mrs. Bedal came out. "Silvia, I'm glad you came. Were you able to get your apple crop in yet?"

"No," Silvia said, looking down. "Thomas hasn't done it yet."

"Has he been drinking and beating you again?" Laura asked quietly.

Silvia shook her head. "He's still drinkin', but he's kept his temper under control."

Laura put her arm around Silvia and walked inside, saying, "If he lays a hand on you again, you and the kids come here to Apple Hill and stay. You'll need to be thinking about going to the sheriff."

The meeting went well, and a response to the Klan was planned. Several agreed to hand out flyers, and the ladies from the south part of the county took Laura's special signs to post along the roads on the way home.

Silvia Leidenburg was the last to leave. Laura knew that she didn't want to go home.

"What can I do for you, Silvia? Are you hungry?" Laura asked, putting her arm around Silvia's shoulder.

"I don't know what to do with him. I just don't," she said, breaking down in tears.

"Where is your husband now? Is he drinking at the house?" Laura asked.

Tears rolled down Silvia's face, "When I left, he was heading back into town. He said he was going to get some supplies, but I know he was going to the saloon. I just know it."

Laura ached for this woman, her neighbor. There was little she could do to change the situation, but she did her best to comfort Silvia. Laura soothed her tears and listened to her broken dreams. When Silvia married Thomas, she never imagined things would change so much, that there would be so much pain in their family.

Finally Silvia calmed down and ran out of words. The two women stood and watched the leaves dance down the lane for a few minutes. Silvia was first to break the silence.

"Thank you for listening, Laura," she said. "I haven't been able to talk to anyone about our problems in a long, long time."

"Well, you know you're welcome in our house any time you need to talk or need a safe place to go," Laura answered.

When Silvia said good-bye, Laura watched her, brow creased with concern, until she disappeared over the hill.

SILVIA TAKES A STAND

While Laura and the women were meeting at Apple Hill, Manly was in Mansfield, putting the supplies he'd gotten from the general store into the back of the wagon. He saw Thomas Leidenburg staggering on the sidewalk.

"Hey, Thomas," he called out, "you need to stop drinking. It's going to kill you and your family."

"Leave my family out of it," Leidenburg snapped.

Manly just shook his head and got up on the bed of the wagon. "Your family will end up leaving you if you don't drink yourself to death first."

"Mind your own business, Wilder."

"Just think about it," Manly said, "before it's too late." He giddiyapped the horses and rode up next to Leidenburg. "You may want to drink yourself to death, but you got no right to take your family along!"

"You're asking for trouble, Wilder. Remember that!"

Manly looked him coldly in the eye. "If I hear of your

hitting your wife and children again, I'll be bringing trouble to *your* door."

"Is that a threat?" Leidenburg sneered.

"No, it's a fact. Hit them again, and you'll have me to fight."

Leidenburg laughed. "I'm not scared of a man with a crippled leg!"

Manly shook his head. "My leg might be lame, but you're just a shell of a man. Won't take but one good leg and two hands to teach you a lesson."

Manly rode off, leaving Leidenburg in his dust.

Leidenburg stopped and closed his eyes, wishing he had the power to stop drinking. It wasn't fun anymore. He had lost control of his life.

For the first time in his life, he admitted it and asked himself, *Can I stop drinking? Can I ever stop*?

He looked toward the saloon and listened to the voices inside telling him to go on. "It will feel so good," they said.

Then he thought about what Manly said about his wife and children. From somewhere deep inside, another voice told him to be strong, to change, to go home.

Leidenburg walked past Tippy's and headed toward the farm. With each step away from the saloon, he felt worse and worse.

He had bought and hidden two more bottles of whiskey in his work bag in the barn. Though he had vowed to stop, he just wanted one more drink. "I'll stop tomorrow," he said as he walked into the barn.

But the bag wasn't there! He tore the barn apart, trying to find it, but he was too late. Silvia had gone through the house and barn, trying to find the hidden bottles that Laura had warned her were somewhere.

Inside the farmhouse, Silvia waited. It was only a matter of time until her husband returned home. He had gone to town with two dollars, and no one would give him any more credit. Silvia had found comfort in Laura's counsel and friendship and the power to help her fight the liquor in control of her husband's body.

When her husband opened the door, Silvia could see the confusion in his eyes. The urge to drink was tearing him apart. No matter how sorry she may have felt for him, this could not go on. It was time to stop the madness before it destroyed her and her children.

"Where's my work bag, woman?" Thomas demanded.

"Is this what you're looking for?" Silvia asked, a bottle in each hand.

Thomas eyed the bottles desperately. "Give me that whiskey! I need it!"

Raising the bottles over her head, she looked at her husband and said with cold determination, "The only thing you need is this!"

She smashed the bottles over the edge of the counter! Whiskey splashed everywhere! Thomas started forward, but she held the broken bottles up to stop him. Janson and Sil crept up behind their mother and clung to her dress.

"You'll not be hurtin' us any longer, Thomas Leidenburg!" Silvia said.

Her husband looked at the sharp-edged bottles in her hand. "You're crazy! I'm going to town!"

Swinging around toward the door, she stopped him in his tracks. "If you walk out that door, we don't want you comin' back. We love you, but we won't allow you to hurt us anymore."

"Don't leave, Daddy," Sil whimpered.

Silvia looked her husband in the eye. "If you stay, we will all stay with you, Thomas, but you've got to want to help yourself. We can't do it for you."

Thomas Leidenburg's world seemed to crash around him. He had lost his pride, his sense of accomplishment, all self-respect. He loved his family and hated himself for the things he had done.

Yes, he could blame the drinking, but the truth was, he didn't want to face himself. Did he have the strength to change? To not drink again? To stop the madness? To come home to the peace his family so deeply deserved?

Thomas fell to his knees, sobbing. Silvia and the children came to his side. "We love you, Thomas," Silvia said quietly. "Things can be different. They really can."

Thomas gripped her hand. "Help me, Silvia. Can you help me?"

"Only God can, Thomas. You don't have to do this alone," she whispered. "And we will stand beside you."

CHAPTER 31

CROSS PURPOSES

Outside of town, the three Klan members pulled a large cross up with ropes until it nearly touched the ceiling of the barn.

"It looks good," said the Klan leader.

"What's the other one for?" the thin man asked, pointing to the smaller, ten-foot cross they'd built.

"That's a little present for that Wilder woman."

"Are we gonna night ride on her?" the stocky man asked.

"We might," the Grand Dragon said, "we just might."

"Might when?" the thin man winked, moving closer.

"I'm thinkin' that we should leave a flamin' message at her farm tomorrow night. Sort of a taste of what's comin' at the rally."

"But everyone will hear about it!" the thin man exclaimed.

"That's the point. A little advertisin' never hurt the cause. In St. Louis, they even put ads in the paper announcin' their rallies."

"Why don't we do that?" the stocky man asked.

"We'll do a lot of things once we get some new recruits. Why, if we had five hundred members, we could rule the Ozarks."

"You'd be like a king," the thin man smiled.

"That's kind of what I have in mind," he winked. "But first we got to clean up Mansfield and shut that Wilder woman up." He walked over to the smaller cross. "Come on. Let's get this thing ready."

It took them just short of an hour to wrap the cross in rags. "Should we soak it with gas now?" the stocky man asked.

The Grand Dragon shook his head. "You don't do that until you're ready to light it. Tomorrow night, we'll soak it good. Then, we'll light up the sky over that apple farm of theirs."

"What's that noise?" the stocky man asked.

They all stopped to listen. "Sounds like bells," the Grand Dragon said. "Sounds like school bells."

They walked to the front of the barn and looked down the road. A caravan of cars and wagons with women ringing bells was coming toward them.

"What in tarnation is that?" the thin man asked.

"Looks like that Wilder woman is up to somethin'," the Grand Dragon said.

As Laura's caravan rode past, one of the women

shouted out, "Keep your children in school! Stand up against the Klan!"

The Grand Dragon spat on the ground. "Get out a can of gas. We're goin' to do a little cross-burnin' tonight."

CHAPTER 32

ROUNDUP

Laura led a caravan of bell-ringing women in wagons and automobiles through the hills and hollows of Wright County, rounding up the children from the fields. Many of the farmers grabbed their children back, but some were so shocked by the ringing bells that they didn't know what to do.

Sheriff Peterson came out on a complaint called in by one of the farmers and warned Laura that she and her friends could be arrested for trespassing. When he conceded that it was the law that children had to go to school, the women cheered and clanged their bells in a deafening victory cheer.

What Laura hadn't anticipated was that there were more children than the school could handle. Since a lot of them had never been to school, Miss O'Conner soon said enough was enough and closed the school to any new students.

Rev. Youngun and Father Walsh opened their

churches for classroom space. The students were divided up and sent to the improvised schools.

At the Leidenburg farm, Janson and Sil were on ladders in the orchards, trying to get the apple crop in before the frost. Thomas Leidenburg looked deathly ill but was working right along beside them.

When Laura came driving up in her Oldsmobile, Janson and Sil didn't want to go to school. Their father looked at Laura and said, "Take 'em to school, where they belong."

Laura got out of her car and walked over to Thomas. "You look ill. You want me to get Dr. George?"

"No," he said, wiping perspiration from his face. "I've just got the shakes."

"We all had a long talk last night. Pa said he's goin' to stop drinkin'," Janson said proudly.

"Oh, Thomas, that's wonderful!" Laura said, hugging him. She looked around at the half-picked orchard. "Your apples are hardly in. You want me to leave Janson and Sil here?"

Barely able to talk and think straight, Leidenburg said, "Can't make an exception for my children." He pushed Sil and Janson toward Laura. "You kids go with Mrs. Wilder. You need schoolin'."

"But Pa," Janson asked, "what about the crop? If we don't get it in before the freeze, we'll lose everything!"

Leidenburg lifted Sil into Laura's car and gave Janson a boost. "I've decided to straighten out my life. What will be will be."

Laura put her hands on Leidenburg's shoulders.

"Thomas, you've taken the first step. The rest will take care of itself."

As a gust of cold wind picked up the leaves around him, Leidenburg coughed, then walked back into the orchard. "I sure hope so, Laura, 'cause my family's all I've got left."

While Laura rounded up the kids, Manly kept up Apple Hill Farm and worked on repairing the school in the afternoons. He recruited Maurice Springer to help on the roof.

Miss O'Conner was leaving for the day when they arrived.

"Going home early, Miss O'Conner?" Manly asked.

"Finished up the next spelling lessons, so now I can go home and grade homework," she said, locking the door.

"Pretty young woman like you should meet some of the bachelors in town," Maurice said.

"Don't have time for tomfoolery. I just want to educate the children as best I can."

Manly took off his tool sack. "Rev. Youngun said the Hardacre boys are doing great in school. You must be a miracle teacher."

"Just because they're from the Hardacres doesn't mean they can't learn," she snapped.

"I didn't mean it like that. 'Course they can learn," said Manly. "It's just that they've come so far and so fast under you."

Miss O'Conner dropped the keys in her purse. "They've won all the spelling bees so far, which I'm very proud of. The other children are going to have to study hard to keep up. There's no magic or trick. Just study hard."

"You and my wife are a lot alike," Manly said, looking at a hammer.

"And how's that?" Miss O'Conner asked.

"You're both stubborn as mules. If you ever got together and worked for a common cause, there'd be no stopping you two."

Miss O'Conner said, "I guess that's a compliment." As she walked down the road toward the Hardacres, Manly set the ladder up in the back and Maurice climbed up.

"I still don't know why we're doin' this by ourselves," Maurice griped. "We don't even have kids in this school!"

"Don't matter," Manly said quietly. "It's the right thing to do. School's good for the whole community."

Maurice shook his head, trying to trick Manly into arguing. "And nothin' wrong with gettin' paid for a day's work, neither."

Manly just laughed. "You'll have to wait for your reward, Maurice."

The roof was full of weak spots and outright holes. Manly showed Maurice a place where you could lift up a shingle and look right down on the teacher's desk.

As they were setting out their tools and nails, Manly pointed to the front of the school. Gene, Red, and Wiley were coming out of the woods. Miss O'Conner was far down the road.

"What those boys doin' 'round here now?" Maurice whispered.

"Let's just see what they're up to," Manly said.

As if they'd done it before, the three boys walked to the side of the building, pushed the trash barrel under the window, climbed up, and jimmied open the window.

"They're breakin' in the school," Maurice whispered. "Think they're going to steal somethin'?"

Manly whispered, "Let's see," and pulled back the shingle.

Below them the three Hardacres boys were carefully looking through the teacher's desk.

"Aha," Wiley said, "I told you she writes up the next day's spelling list each day before she goes back to my house."

"Is this how you taught us all the words before the last spellin' bee?" Red asked.

"Yup," Wiley said, very proud of himself. "I used my brain. This way we're sure to win the money at the end of the spelling contest next week."

Wiley copied the list, then they left the way they came in.

As they walked away, Manly looked at Maurice. "Think we got a case of the cheatin' bees in the spelling bee."

They worked on the roof until dark and were putting their tools away when Sheriff Peterson came riding up on his horse. "Manly, is that you up there?"

"Yup, it's me. What do you want, Sheriff?"

"You need to get on home right now!" the sheriff said, holding back his horse.

A chill went through Manly. "Is something wrong? Is Laura all right?"

"The Klan burned a cross at Apple Hill," the sheriff said bluntly.

Manly and Maurice packed up their tools and took the back paths to Apple Hill Farm. On the highest ridge overlooking their property was a ten-foot burning cross.

Laura arrived at the same time, and her mood of elation at rounding up some of the children turned dark.

"Who did this, Sheriff? Did you catch them?" Laura demanded.

"Pretty obvious, it's the Klan's work. Word's out they're upset with you and have called a rally come Friday night," the sheriff said, the blazing cross reflecting in his eyes.

"Come on, Maurice. Let's get it down," Manly said.

"They're claiming to be protecting the farmers' harvest and the schools," the sheriff said.

While Manly and Maurice pulled the burning cross down and stamped out the gas-soaked beams, Laura turned to the sheriff. "They're not speaking for the farmers, Sheriff. They're speaking for fear, ignorance, and misery. Nothing more."

CHAPTER 33

FARMER'S ALMANAC SAYS

hough there was a chill in the air, Laura was still hot about the Klan cross burned on Apple Hill property. Summers had come out and told her about the pressure the Klan had put upon him, and the sheriff was keeping watch on both the newspaper office and the farm.

Of course being a one-man sheriff's department made the job difficult, but he was doing his job as best he could.

It seemed that all day Thursday, no matter where Laura went, people were talking about two things: the Klan rally on Friday evening and what the *Farmer's Almanac* was predicting.

Lafayette Bedal stood in front of his general store, talking to Laura and Manly. "*Farmer's Almanac* says it's going to freeze, maybe snow come Sunday."

Manly kicked his shoe against the wooden walk. "We got all our crops in and the orchards picked. Most everyone has by now, I suppose."

Lafayette shook his head. "Some folks wait until the last minute. I hear there's several crews of men workin' 'round the clock over in the next county, bringing in the crops for late farmers."

Laura said sarcastically, "I suppose it's my fault they waited too long?"

"No," Lafayette said, "but those farmers who don't get their crops in on time will sure be lookin' for someone to blame."

Sheriff Peterson walked by on his rounds and waved. "Any more trouble last night?"

"No, Sheriff, everything was calm," Manly said. "Thanks for keepin' an eye on things."

"How many Klan members are there in this county, Laura?" Lafayette asked.

Laura sighed. "Summers said he's only seen three of them, but he says there's a Grand Dragon and . . ."

Manly interrupted her. "Dragons, sheets, and burnin' crosses—sounds like a couple of escaped lunatics from the St. Louis mental hospital."

"Don't say that too loud," Lafayette cautioned. "Folks say they're everywhere."

"We'll see tomorrow night, won't we?" Laura said.

"If there's more than a handful of half-wits in bed-sheets, I'll be surprised," Manly said.

"I don't know," Lafayette cautioned. "They could be anyone in town by day and Klansmen at night."

"Don't let your imagination run wild," Laura said. "Come on, Manly. We've got some more shopping to do."

While Laura and Manly went to pick up meat and
vegetables at the other stores, Stephen Scales, the
town's telegraph operator and master of the train sta-
tion, loaded a large box onto his wagon. It was simply
addressed:

From: Sears, Roebuck and Company
        Chicago, Ill.

To: Terry Youngun
        Mansfield, Missouri

Scales couldn't guess what was in it, but when Terry
saw the box, he knew instantly!

"Larry, come quick. I got you a present."

"What is it, Terry?" Larry said.

As his little brother cut the box open with his trusty
pocketknife, Larry suddenly felt a twinge of guilt. The
thought of Terry thinking enough of him to send away
for a present choked him up.

"You're going to like this," Terry said, cutting down
the package's side.

Larry tried to imagine what it could be. A basketball,
a baseball, a saddle?

"Yup," Terry said as he cut open the other side, "this
is something that will make you feel better." He
stopped and looked at Larry. "Matter of fact, you might
even call the present I got for you 'eye medicine.' "

"Eye medicine?" Terry exclaimed. "In that box?"

Terry lifted out the new pair of boxing gloves. "If you keep your dukes up, these will keep your eyes open."

Though Larry was reluctant, he put on the gloves and went into the barn. For the rest of the afternoon, he was coached by Terry on how to hit the punching bag.

"Go on! Smack 'em! Smack Red!" Terry yelled, swinging around and punching the air himself.

Larry looked over and stopped. "If you know so much about fightin' and boxin', why are you always hidin' behind me when Red comes at you?"

"You're the older brother and supposed to protect me," Terry said, nodding his head.

Larry began to punch and jab again while Terry yelled from the side. "Just pretend the bag is Red Shaughnessy. Get mad," Terry said, standing next to his brother like a fight coach. "Hit him in the face."

Larry punched and talked. "I'm just doing this for the exercise. I don't want to fight, 'cause fightin's not right."

Terry shook his head. "What would you rather have, two black eyes and all your teeth knocked out and be right? Or have a little guilt from knockin' Red's block off?"

CHAPTER 34

KLAN RALLY

By Friday afternoon the people of the town were treating the upcoming Klan rally as a circus event. Everyone was going, just to see what happened.

Some of the families had even packed picnic lunches and gone out to the old ballfield on the edge of town to pick a good spot to watch. The Klan had gotten there before daybreak and left a large cross, draped in rags, laying on the ground behind an old wagon which was to be the podium.

By nightfall, there were even kids selling hot dogs and lemonade, and a photographer had set up a backdrop and was taking pictures of people. There wasn't much to do in Mansfield, so the people there took any opportunity to gather together.

Laura had called a meeting at Apple Hill Farm that afternoon and organized the women's response to the Klan rally. She and her friends didn't treat the meeting as an event. They saw it for what it was—an insult to the people of the town.

After woman after woman spoke, expressing their disdain for the Klan, Laura got up to express herself.

"This town is too small for big hatreds like this," Laura said to the assembled women in her living room. "If we allow a cancer like this to take hold, life in Mansfield will never be the same. It will soon be neighbor against neighbor and brother against brother."

The sound of clapping coming from outside the house startled Laura and the other women. Standing on the porch and in the yard was Father Walsh and a group of women from the Hardacres.

Father Walsh came into the living room. "Laura Wilder, I've brought you some more Christian soldiers."

Laura smiled. "Father Walsh, you and the women of the Hardacres are welcome. We all have a common enemy in the Klan."

"Amen to that," Father Walsh said.

When all the new helpers were in the house, Laura took the floor again to plan their response. As she started to speak, the front door opened.

Laura didn't pay it much heed and said, "If you're coming in, come on in. We need all the help we can get."

Miss O'Conner stepped into the living room. "Even if I'm Irish?" she asked with a simple smile.

"Especially if you're Irish," Laura laughed. "Come on in, Miss O'Conner. We need you to help lead this class."

They worked up a plan and agreed to meet at the schoolhouse at six o'clock, which was an hour before the scheduled rally.

"Be sure to bring your bells," Laura shouted from the front porch as the women were leaving. Laura went down the stairs and touched Miss O'Conner on the arm. "I'm so glad you came. It means a lot to all of us to have the support of the people of the Hardacres."

Maurene looked at Laura. "The Klan is not just against the Irish. They're against all immigrants in this country made up of immigrants. And they're not just against Catholics; they're against everybody who's different from them."

"I'm sorry this had to be your introduction to America," Laura said quietly.

"Every country has evil people. They just go by different names," Miss O'Conner said.

Father Walsh came up behind them. "If you two don't stop talking, the Klan rally will be over before we get there."

He told them that the Buchanans of his parish and the Leidenburgs of Rev. Youngun's congregation were the only two families who hadn't gotten in their apple crops yet.

"What should we do about it?" Miss O'Conner asked.

Father Walsh smiled. "Rev. Youngun and I have worked out a plan where we'll lead our congregations into the fields after morning service to—how did Rev. Youngun say it—bring in the . . . ?"

"Sheaves," Laura laughed. "The song says, 'We will go rejoicing, bringing in the sheaves.' "

When Father Walsh walked over to crank up his car,

Miss O'Conner turned to Laura and said, "Your husband is a good man."

"I think so," Laura said, not knowing where the conversation was going.

"He and his friend Maurice have been working almost every afternoon repairing the school. You must be very proud that he believes so much in what you write."

"Oh, I am proud of him," Laura smiled, now understanding what Manly had been up to each afternoon.

Miss O'Conner laughed. "And he told me that you and I are a lot alike."

"What's so funny about that?" Laura asked.

"Oh, it's not funny," Miss O'Conner chuckled. "I think it's pretty accurate."

"Well, I hope he said that we were both smart and easy to get along with," Laura responded, half in jest.

Maurene turned and said over her shoulder, "Actually, he said we were both 'stubborn as mules.' Goodbye, Mrs. Wilder."

After the women and Father Walsh had all left Apple Hill Farm, Manly hitched up the buggy and drove Laura to the school. There was a cold wind in the air. As they road along the county road, leaves flew in circles and dust devils crossed the road.

"Stubborn as mules?" Laura asked.

"What?" Manly asked.

"You said that Miss O'Conner and I were a lot alike because we are both 'stubborn as mules.'"

Manly giddiyapped the horses and chuckled. "Sometimes the truth hurts, don't it, girl?" He laughed. "I think I'll start callin' you the mule sisters, since you both got some red in your hair!"

"How's the new roof coming on the school?" she asked without looking at him.

Manly laughed and put his arm around Laura, who kissed him on the cheek.

Later, on the old ballfield, about half the town was sitting on blankets and chairs, waiting for the rally to begin. The field was half-lit by lanterns and torches brought by the townspeople. There was a nervous feeling in the air, just as children get when they're doing something naughty.

From behind the wagon, six hooded figures appeared. They poured gasoline on the rag-draped cross and raised it into the air. One of them picked up an old battle drum and began a slow, rhythmic beat.

A hooded figure stepped up onto the back of the old wagon and shouted to the crowd, "People of Mansfield, the Klan of the Ozarks has come to protect the farmers of Wright County from those who want to destroy their harvest, and to keep American education for Americans."

A few people in the crowd clapped.

The hooded figure continued. "You are privileged to have in your presence the Grand Dragon of the Ozarks."

As the hooded figure turned around, a match was struck and the cross burst into flames. Burning torches were placed at the corners of the wagon. The speaker jumped off and stood with his arms crossed in front of the wagon.

With the burning cross as a backdrop, a taller hooded figure with a bright red cross painted on his robe climbed up on the wagon. He raised his hands for silence.

"The Klan of the Ozarks has come to Mansfield to help you fight the foreign agents of anti-Americanism. There are people who write articles to take your children away from you and place them under the control of citizens of another country."

The drum beat louder and the pace increased.

The Grand Dragon continued. "American farms should be worked by farm families. Kids can always go to school, but a harvest comes in only once a year."

More people in the crowd applauded.

"But when they go to school, who should teach them? Foreigners? People who aren't Americans?"

Some of the crowd were nodding their heads in agreement, but most were just nodding their heads because they saw someone else do it. A sheep mentality was sweeping the crowd.

The Grand Dragon pointed to the burning cross. "That old rugged cross stands tall for American Christians. It is a symbol of the good Christians of America who built this country and are now losing it to foreigners."

A couple of Scandinavians in the crowd stood up and cheered. Lafayette Bedal shouted from the side of the field, "Sit down, you fools! It's only been a decade since *you* arrived at Ellis Island."

The laughter in the crowd upset the Grand Dragon. "Who was that speaking?" he demanded, pointing toward Lafayette Bedal.

"Lafayette Bedal," someone in the crowd replied.

"Lafayette is your name, huh? Sounds like a Frenchie, if you ask me," the Grand Dragon sneered.

"French Canadian, to be precise," Lafayette shouted back. "And where be *you* from, stranger?"

Raising his hands over his head, the Grand Dragon shouted to the crowd, "I am one-hundred percent American. My relatives helped ring the Liberty Bell and . . ."

From behind the ridge came the sound of bells, softly at first, then getting louder and louder. The Klansmen looked at one another and turned toward the Grand Dragon, who was just as bewildered.

Laura and Miss O'Conner came into view, leading thirty bell-ringing women. The Grand Dragon tried to speak, but was drowned out by the bells. The bell-ringing women walked right through the crowd and stopped in front of the wagon.

Laura held up her hands and the bells stopped. "It's not Halloween yet, so why don't you and the other costumed creatures crawl back under the rock you came out from?"

The Grand Dragon pointed his finger and screamed, "This is the evil agent who has been trying to destroy your school and ruin the harvest!"

A gust of cold wind whipped through the crowd, picking up the robes of the Klan and threatening to put out the torches. Laura tried to climb up on the wagon and was boosted up by some of the women.

Laura looked at the hooded figure. "If you're so proud to be an American, why do you hide behind that hood?"

The Grand Dragon turned to the crowd. "The robes and hoods are symbols that we are the invisible protectors of people for the American way."

"You call yourself a 'one-hundred-percent American,' but you sure don't sound like an Indian. They're the only one-hundred-percent Americans that I've ever known."

Shaking with rage, the Grand Dragon screamed, "This woman is covering up her true motives. She . . ."

Laura stepped over and pulled his hood off. "Speaking of covers, this bedsheet you're wearing needs washing!"

Summers recognized the dark-haired stranger who had threatened him at his office. He aimed his camera at the Grand Dragon and shouted, "Hey, Dragon! Smile." When the Grand Dragon turned his head, he was blinded by the bright burst of the flash.

"Print that on the front page of tomorrow's paper," Laura laughed.

"I'll caption it, 'Dragon beheaded,'" Summers chuckled.

The crowd was laughing and had gathered in front of

the wagon, now clearly on Laura's side. The five Klansmen on the ground huddled together, nervous at how outnumbered they were.

"You people are not wanted in our town," Laura shouted. "Get out before we do to you what you've done to others."

Laura grabbed the Dragon's arm and walked him off the stage. The crowd pushed the six Klan members from the field while the women clanged their bells.

Turning to the burning cross, Laura shouted above the clanging of the bells, "No one has a right to misuse religion this way. It should be pulled down now."

Manly and Maurice had been waiting for Laura's cue. They looped ropes over the top of the cross and pulled it to the ground. As they stamped out the flames, the field darkened and the clanging of the bells faded out.

A cold wind whipped through the crowd. Two of the four torches around the wagon went out. Laura raised her hands for silence.

"I've been accused of trying to destroy the apple harvest. That was never my intention. What I wanted was for the children of this county—for every child in the country—to go to school for a harvest of their minds.

"But I want to confess that my emotions took control of my reason. You can't change things overnight. Farmers of this county have been keeping their children home during harvest time for generations. And unless the harvest is in, they won't be able to feed their families."

Pausing for a moment, Laura looked over at Manly,

who winked back at her. "If we can all work toward a goal of educating the children and keeping them in school *except* during the harvest times, it is the first step toward really producing opportunities for these children of promise that we all love so dearly."

Another burst of wind whipped through the ballfield, taking out one of the last two torches on the wagon.

"The *Farmer's Almanac* says that there is a hard freeze or even snow due here Monday, and I understand that two families have not gotten all their apples in yet." Farmers in the crowd looked around, trying to figure out who was in that predicament. "Rev. Youngun and Father Walsh have come up with a plan, which I want them both to tell you about." Laura turned to the two men of the cloth.

Father Walsh said, "We've got two families in the community who haven't completely picked their orchards yet—the Buchanan family in my parish and the Leidenburgs over in Rev. Youngun's parish."

Rev. Youngun laughed. "That's 'congregation,' not 'parish,' Father. Folks, we need your help. Come to Sunday service dressed to help in the fields after service."

Father Walsh said, "So far we've got the Catholics helping the Buchanans and the Protestants helping the Leidenburgs. But as far as we're concerned, if you Protestants need help, we've got some extra lads with strong hands."

"I think that's the sentiment of the whole community," Laura said. "Good neighbors helping good neighbors."

A cheer broke out among the farmers, and the bell-ringing women clanged their approval. While Rev. Youngun and Father Walsh spoke to small groups around them, instructing them on the tools that were going to be needed, another freezing wind flew across the ridge.

Laura could feel the temperature dropping and thought about what the *Farmer's Almanac* said. Monday was just two days away. Laura hoped the freeze wasn't going to come a day early.

CHAPTER 35

BRINGING IN THE SHEAVES

I t was an emotional service at Rev. Youngun's church, as packed as if it were Easter. For the first time the congregation could remember, Thomas Leidenburg joined his wife and children in their pew. His hands no longer shook, and his voice rang out clearly through all the hymns. At the end of the service, the entire congregation stood and cheered as Thomas Leidenburg walked down the aisle with his family, smiling through tears of joy.

Once everyone was assembled outside the church, Rev. Youngun led his congregation down the road to the Leidenburgs', singing "Bringing in the Sheaves."

Across the hill, Father Walsh was speaking in Latin, leading a solemn procession of worshipers to the Buchanans'.

Miss O'Conner lifted her veil at the sound of the Protestants' joyful singing and whispered to Father Walsh. "Listen to them sing," Maurene said. "Let's leave the Latin behind. None of these people know what you're saying, anyway."

He feigned indignation, then laughed, "Well, what song do you have in mind?"

"How about 'When Irish Eyes Are Smiling'?"

"Well, why don't you lead?" Father Walsh said.

Miss O'Conner hesitated and then began the song. Father Walsh joined in, and soon all were happily singing away.

As they spread out to bring in the Buchanans' apple crop, Miss O'Conner looked across the hill to where Rev. Youngun's group was working. She quietly slipped away and walked toward the Leidenburg farm.

Rev. Youngun laughed when he heard the singing coming across the hill. "Well, I'll be, that doesn't sound like Latin to me!"

Manly looked at Laura. "Bet your mule sister had a hand in that," he whispered.

"Manly," she said, "I don't like that 'mule sister' stuff."

Manly chuckled and walked away. While the people began bringing in the Leidenburgs' apple crop, Summers came racing up in his automobile.

Summers tossed a newspaper to Laura. "Hot off the press! How do you like the headline?"

Laura opened the paper. Bannered across the front was the headline, "Dragon Beheaded" and a half-page photo of Laura and the Grand Dragon with his hood off.

"Were you able to identify him?" Laura asked.

"I handled this story myself. Found out there's an

arrest warrant out on him in St. Louis, so Sheriff Peterson picked him up on the north road."

"Can I see a copy?" asked Miss O'Conner, who had just arrived. She took a copy from the seat of Summers' car.

Rev. Youngun walked up and listened from the side. For the first time, he noticed how pretty Miss O'Conner was. She glanced over at him, then looked down, blushing.

Laura took Summers by the arm. "Andrew Jackson Summers, I want to introduce you to Miss Maurene O'Conner, the new teacher at the Mansfield school you were so interested in."

Summers stammered, "Ple . . . pleased to meet you, ma'am."

"She's Laura's mule sister," Manly laughed.

"Mule sister? I don't understand," Summers said with raised eyebrows.

"Hush, Manly," Laura chuckled. "How do you like the headline?" she asked Miss O'Conner.

"I couldn't have written it better myself," she said, winking at Summers.

While the others spoke among themselves, Rev. Youngun walked up and introduced himself to Miss O'Conner. Laura, always curious, listened in.

"You're the father of those three children in the class, aren't you?" Miss O'Conner asked.

Rev. Youngun smiled. "Yes, there's my oldest, Larry, who . . ."

"Who's been getting into fights," Miss O'Conner injected.

Rev. Youngun said, "There's another side to that one you're not seeing, but we'll discuss that later. And there's my daughter, Sherry, who . . ."

Miss O'Conner laughed. "Who likes to sing and pray."

"That's the one," Rev. Youngun chuckled. "And there's my middle child, Terry. He's a bundle."

A screaming girl raced by, with Terry hot on her heels, trying to pull her pigtails.

Miss O'Conner said, "From the look of that hair, I still think he's got a touch of the Irish in him."

Rev. Youngun smiled. "As a matter of fact, my grandmother was from Ireland. Came over in 1836."

Miss O'Conner's eyes widened. "So I was right, the lad has a bit of the Emerald Isle in his blood." She turned to look at Terry, who was racing by again, then said, "I bet your wife loves them very much."

"She did," Rev. Youngun said, looking down.

"Did?"

"Norma passed away last year," Rev. Youngun said quietly.

"I'm sorry. I didn't know," she stumbled.

Manly caught the last part of the conversation and stepped in. "I got something to talk to the teacher about for a moment, Rev. Youngun, if you don't mind."

Manly took Miss O'Conner by the arm, walked her to the edge of the orchard, and told her about the three boys from the Hardacres who had copied down her spelling list.

Laura came up and stood beside Rev. Youngun. She noticed him looking at Miss O'Conner with a glint in his eye.

"She's a pretty woman, isn't she?"

"She sure is. Too bad she's Catholic," he said to himself.

"Stranger things have happened than two people of different religions falling in love," Laura chuckled.

"Love?" Rev. Youngun stammered. "I was only . . ."

"Rev. Youngun, you need a mother for those three children of yours."

Sherry Youngun ran by, screaming like a wild Indian. Terry was chasing her with a toad in his hand. Larry was trying to catch Terry, to keep him from hurting the toad.

Laura started again. "As I was saying, you need a mother for those three children and . . ."

Rev. Youngun interrupted her this time. "You're right," he said, watching his three children run in a circle around them.

A few flakes of snow floated over the orchard, spurring the people to pick faster. Laura wondered, "How does the *Farmer's Almanac* do it?"

As the temperature dropped, Laura worried that they wouldn't get the apple crop in on time.

Then from across the hill, Father Walsh and the rest of his flock came singing "When Irish Eyes Are Smiling." He brought his people to a halt in front of Laura and Rev. Youngun.

"You Protestants need any help?" Father Walsh laughed.

The combined forces brought in the apples as the temperature dropped and the snow flurries increased. By evening, all the apples were safely stored away.

CHAPTER 36

THE FINAL ROUND

While Laura and Summers sat quietly in the back of the classroom, working on a follow-up story about the new teacher, Manly and Maurice were up on the roof, trying to finish before a heavy snow came.

They'd only gotten about a half-inch of snow on Sunday night, but the *Farmer's Almanac* had been right; the freeze had come. If they hadn't worked as a community, they would have never gotten in all the crops.

The three boys from the Hardacres were having a tough time with the spelling words. They couldn't understand it! Each of them had copied the words from the list in the teacher's desk, but the words Miss O'Conner asked were completely different.

Though Larry had practiced sounding out words at home, he fell out in the final round of the spelling bee. Janson Leidenburg, who had only been back in school for three days, won the spelling bee and the prize money.

Laura walked over and whispered in his ear, "Janson, I'm so proud of you."

"I did it for my father," Janson said, smiling.

Miss O'Conner clapped for attention, and Laura went back to her seat beside Summers.

"I think we all have learned several lessons from this spelling bee and from the past several weeks of school," Miss O'Conner said.

"Like what?" Frenchie asked.

"Well, for one thing, I've learned that you can't judge people by different standards." Seeing the blank look on some of the children's faces, Miss O'Conner explained. "What I mean is, just because a child is Irish or Chinese or white or . . . or Catholic or Protestant does not mean that child is any better or any worse than anyone else."

She walked to the side of the room. "I've also learned that America is different from other countries, because it is made up of people from all countries of the world. It is a group of immigrants who have come together to form a common memory and heritage that is and will be truly unique to the world."

Pointing to the copy of the Constitution of the United States on the wall, she tapped Wiley on the shoulder. "Read that line, Wiley."

Wiley looked at it carefully and then said, "All men are created equal."

"That's right," Miss O'Conner said, "and though it is still just a goal that this country is working toward, it is the truth."

"And what about girls?" asked Missouri Poole.

"And girls are created equal too," Miss O'Conner said, walking over to the blackboard. "I have also learned that punishment should be handed out equally, so Wiley, Red, and Gene, come to the blackboard, please."

The three bewildered Hardacre boys stood up and slowly inched forward. "What'd we do, Miss O'Conner?" Red asked.

"I think you boys know what you did. Do you want to confess?"

"For the love of Ireland, Miss O'Conner," Wiley whimpered, "we've done nothing wrong except protect your good name and our church."

"Leave the church out of this," Miss O'Conner said. "What you did has nothing to do with the church, except that you boys need to go take confession with Father Walsh." She took out her paddle and whacked it on her hand several times. "Tell me how you've been getting the spelling words in advance."

Red protested, "We studied hard and . . ."

From the ceiling came Manly's voice. He had pulled back the shingle and looked down on the classroom. "Tell the truth, boy. You never know who might have been watching you."

"Yeah, you never know," said Maurice through a smaller hole in the roof.

All three boys blurted out the story at the same time and stood there with their heads hanging down. They jumped when Miss O'Conner hit the paddle on the side of her desk.

Gene's eyes went as round as saucers. "But you said equal punishment! You only made them write on the blackboard!"

"That I did, that I did," Miss O'Conner said. "While I dismiss the class early, I want each of you to write on the board one hundred times, 'I will not cheat.' "

"One hundred times!" protested Wiley.

"Okay, you write it one hundred and ten times!" The teacher turned to the other two. "Do you two have any comments?"

"No ma'am!" they said simultaneously.

Miss O'Conner watched as they began writing their punishment. "Defending the church, were you? Why, did you know that St. Patrick said his prayers, day and night, immersed in cold water up to his neck? Now *that's* defending the church!"

She turned to the other students, who were giggling with glee over their punishment, "Class dismissed!"

The children cheered and rushed from their desks and benches. Terry picked up his carry sack and slipped behind Red. "Hey, Red, think you know which end of the chalk to use?"

Red turned around and stared at him. Terry threw air punches and soon found himself picked up in the air by his belt loops.

Summers held him up in the air and said, "My son told me you'd been pickin' the fights for your brother to fight. One day, redhead, you're going to get your block knocked off."

When his feet hit the ground, Terry ran out the door like a rabbit. He caught up with the Youngun gang halfway to the Willow Creek Bridge.

The gang spent the next hour skipping stones on the creek, laughing about the Hardacres boys getting caught.

"Uh-oh," Little James said from the rail of the bridge. "Trouble's coming."

Red, Wiley, and Gene were running down the road as fast as they could come. Terry ran back to get his carry sack.

Red came toward Terry. "I've had enough of your lip, shrimp!"

Larry stepped forward. "I'll talk to my brother about his wise mouth. You leave him alone."

"Get out of my way, preacher's son. I've already given you two black eyes," Red said, pressing forward.

"Let me at him. Let me at him!" Terry screamed, dancing forward with the new boxing gloves on. "I'll tear him apart," he shouted. "I'll beat him to a pulp."

The kids just stopped and stared, because the boxing gloves were bigger than his arms! It was a wonder he could even lift them above his head! He looked like a rooster jumping around, punching the air.

Larry thought it was time for his brother to learn a lesson. "Okay, Terry, it's your fight."

Terry went white as a ghost as his brother stepped

back and Red stepped forward. "But, but, Larry, I thought . . ."

"I know exactly what you thought," Larry said. "You took it for granted that I'd defend you."

Red chased Terry around the bridge, but it was like David and Goliath—only this David was running for dear life! Larry watched carefully, not wanting it to go too far, but even he laughed as his brother ducked between Red's legs and landed a punch on Red's behind.

Terry stopped and looked at the glove. He'd actually landed a punch!

"Okay, enough's enough," Larry said. "Fight's over."

Since Manly hadn't finished the roof and Laura wanted to leave, Summers had agreed to give her a ride to Apple Hill in his car. Since they were going near the Hardacres, Miss O'Conner got into the back seat.

As they got near the Willow Creek Bridge, where the road divided, Laura saw the kids gathered around. "Wonder what's going on?"

Miss O'Conner shook her head. "I thought there was trouble coming from the way that Red took off. I'm sure they're fighting again."

Summers pulled the car off to the edge of the road and said, "Let's walk up quietly and see what's really going on this time."

On the bridge, Terry scampered onto the rail. Larry said again, "The fight's over, Red."

Red stood his ground. "Fight's not over until I say it's over. It's your turn," he sneered, tossing a wild punch above Larry's head.

"I said I didn't want to fight," Larry warned.

Red swung again, and Larry stepped out of the way. "Come on, preacher's son. Are you chicken?"

"I'm warning you, I don't want to fight you, Red Shaughnessy."

Red dashed forward, swinging wildly. Larry sidestepped him and tripped Red to the ground. Like a raging bull, Red got up again and charged. Larry jumped aside and pushed Red down again.

"Stop it, Red," Larry said, looking at the exhausted boy on the ground. "There's no need to fight."

"All it takes is one good punch," Red said, getting to his feet, "and I'll knock your lights out."

Red charged forward, but Larry was too quick and sidestepped out of the way. Unable to stop, Red hit the side of the bridge and broke through!

Some of the kids started laughing as Red hit the deep water, but Gene Buchanan screamed, "Red can't swim! He'll drown!"

Larry jumped through the broken railing and hit the ice-cold water. Red was struggling. The weight of his wet clothes was pulling him down.

"Help! Help!" he blubbered, going under the water again.

Larry swam over and grabbed Red's shoulder, spinning him around. He put a headlock around Red and pulled him stroke by stroke to the edge of the creek.

The children standing on the edge pulled Red to shore. As Larry stepped onto the bank and knelt down beside Red, Summers caught it with the flash of his camera.

"You're a hero, boy!" Summers said. "You're an honest-to-goodness hero!"

Miss O'Conner put her hand on Larry's shoulder. "You're a brave lad. I'm sorry I was wrong and accused you of starting a fight with Red."

Red coughed up water and looked at Larry. "You didn't have to do it, Youngun, but thanks. I owe you."

"I did what I had to do, Red," Larry said, reaching out his hand.

Sweet came down the bank to see what the commotion was all about. He was carrying his "porcupine eggs" in his wicker cage. When he saw Terry, he got really excited.

"Hey, Terry," he shouted, "can I trade these porcupine eggs for some of Davy Crockett's hair like you sold to Li?"

Miss O'Conner laughed. "Porcupine eggs and Davy Crockett's hair? Really, Mr. Terry Youngun, I think there's a bit of the blarney in you!"

Laura swung Terry off his feet and ruffled his auburn hair. "A bit, Miss O'Conner? Why, from the looks of this hair and the tales he tells, I think we've got a real live leprechaun on our hands."

Terry struggled free and ran behind Larry.

"What 'bout my porcupine eggs?" Sweet asked again.

"Go sit on 'em 'till they hatch," Terry said, scampering up the bank.

About the Author

T. L. Tedrow is a best-selling author, screenwriter, and film producer. His books include the eight-book "Days of Laura Ingalls Wilder Series": *Missouri Homestead, Children of Promise, Good Neighbors, Home to the Prairie, The World's Fair, Mountain Miracle, The Great Debate,* and *Land of Promise,* which are the basis of a new television series. His four-book series on The Younguns, to be released in 1993, has also been sold as a television series. His first bestseller, *Death at Chappaquiddick,* has been made into a feature film. He lives with his wife, Carla, and four children in Winter Park, Florida.